MADAME ROSA

"Come here, Momo."

"Now what? You're not going to conk out again?"

"I hope not. But if this goes on, they're going to put me in the hospital. I don't want to go. I'm sixty-seven . . ."

"Sixty-nine."

"All right, sixty-eight. So listen to me, Momo. I don't want to go to the hospital. For thirty-five years I gave my ass to the customers, and I'm not giving it to the doctors now. Promise?"

"I promise, Madame Rosa."

"*Khaïrem*?"

"*Khaïrem.*"

MADAME ROSA

EMILE AJAR

TRANSLATED BY RALPH MANHEIM
(Originally published in hardcover as MOMO)

A BERKLEY BOOK
published by
BERKLEY PUBLISHING CORPORATION

They said: "Thou hast gone mad and for the sake
of Him whom thou lovest."
I said: "It is only for the mad that life has savor."

Yāfi'ī, Rawudh al rāyahīn

Translation Copyright © 1977,
by Doubleday & Company, Inc.
Front cover artwork Copyright © 1978
by Atlantic Distributing Corporation
(Published in hardcover
by Doubleday & Company, Inc., as MOMO)

Published by arrangement with Doubleday & Company, Inc.

Doubleday & Company, Inc.
245 Park Avenue
New York, New York 10017

SBN 425-04036-4

BERKLEY BOOKS are published by
Berkley Publishing Corporation
200 Madison Avenue
New York, N. Y. 10016

BERKLEY BOOK® TM 757,375

Printed in the United States of America

Berkley Edition, APRIL, 1979

THE FIRST THING I HAVE TO TELL YOU
is that we lived on the seventh-floor walk-up, so
you can take my word for it that Madame Rosa,
with all the pounds she had to lug around with
her, had more than her share of daily life with all
its sorrows and cares. She said so too, whenever
she wasn't complaining about something else,
because to make matters worse she was Jewish.
Her health wasn't so good either, and I can tell
you right now that if ever a woman deserved an
elevator it was Madame Rosa.

I must have been three when I saw her for the
first time. Younger than that there's no memory,
you live in ignorance. I stopped being ignorant
when I was three or four, and I sometimes miss it.

There were plenty of other Jews, Arabs and
blacks in Belleville, but Madame Rosa had to
climb those six flights all alone. She often told us
she'd die on the stairs some day, and all the kids
would start crying, because that's what you do
when somebody dies. There were six or seven of us
up there; sometimes more.

At first I didn't know that Madame Rosa only
took care of me because of the money order that
came at the end of the month. I didn't find out
until I was six or seven, and it gave me a bad shock

to hear I was paid for. I thought Madame Rosa loved me free gratis and there was some connection between us. I cried about it all one night, and that was my first big sorrow.

Seeing I was sad, Madame Rosa explained that family doesn't mean a thing and told me how some people tie their dogs to a tree and go off on vacation, so every year three thousand dogs die from being deprived of parental affection. Then she picked me up on her lap and swore she loved me more than anything in the world, but I couldn't help thinking of the money order, so I started crying and ran away.

I went to Monsieur Driss's café on the ground floor and sat down across the table from Monsieur Hamil, who sold carpets all over France and had seen everything under the sun. Monsieur Hamil has beautiful eyes that make people feel good all around him. He was very old when I first met him and since then he's just kept getting older.

"Monsieur Hamil, how come you're always smiling?"

"That's my way of thanking God every day for my good memory, little Momo."

My name is Mohammed, but everybody calls me Momo, because it sounds littler.

"Sixty years ago, when I was young, I met a young woman who loved me and I loved her too. It lasted eight months. Then she was sent to a different house, and now, sixty years later, I still remember the day. I said to her: I will never forget you. The years passed and I didn't forget her. Sometimes I was afraid, because I still had a lot of life ahead of me, and how could a poor man like me be sure of his word, when it's God who holds the eraser? But now I don't have to worry. I won't forget Djamila. I have so little time left, I'll die first."

I thought of Madame Rosa. Then after hesitating a while I asked:

"Monsieur Hamil, can somebody live without love?"

He didn't answer. I took a sip of mint tea, which is good for the health. Monsieur Hamil had started wearing a gray djellaba lately, because in case God called him he didn't want to be caught in a business suit. He looked at me and didn't say a word. I guess he thought certain things were no admittance to underage minors. I must have been seven or eight at the time, I can't be exactly sure because I wasn't dated, as you'll see when we're better acquainted if you think it's worth your trouble.

"Monsieur Hamil, why don't you say something?"

"You're very young, and when somebody's very young there are things he'd better not know."

"Monsieur Hamil, can somebody live without love?"

"Yes," he said, and bowed his head in shame.

I burst into tears.

For a long time I didn't know I was an Arab, because nobody insulted me. I only found out when I went to school. But I never got into fights. It always hurts when you hit somebody.

Madame Rosa was Jewish when she was born in Poland, but she'd peddled her ass for several years in Morocco and Algeria and spoke Arabic as well as you or me. She knew Yiddish too for the same reasons and we often spoke that language together. Most of the other tenants in the building were black. There are three black lodging houses on the rue Bisson and two more where they live in tribes like in Africa. The most important are the Sarakollé, and then come the Toucouleurs who are no slouches either. There's plenty of other tribes on the rue Bisson, but I haven't time to list them all. The rest of the street and the Boulevard de Belleville is mostly Jews and Arabs. It goes on that way as far as the Goutte d'Or; then the French population starts in.

At first I didn't know I had no mother. I didn't even know you had to have one. Madame Rosa kept off the subject because she didn't want to give me any ideas. I don't know how I came to be born or exactly what went wrong. My buddy Le Mahoute, who's a few years older than me, told me it comes from hygienic conditions. He was born in Algiers, in the Casbah, and didn't come to France until later. In those days they didn't have hygiene in the Casbah, and he was born because there wasn't any bidet or drinking water or anything. Le Mahoute heard about it later on, when his father tried to convince him that he wasn't to blame and swore that no one had meant any harm. Le Mahoute told me that nowadays whores have a pill for hygiene, but that he was born too soon.

Quite a few mothers came to Madame Rosa's once or twice a week, but always for the other kids. Practically all of them were whores, and when they left town for a few months to work in the provinces, they came to see their kids before and after. That's what started me worrying about my mother. Everybody seemed to have one but me. I began getting stomach cramps and convulsions to make her come and see me. On the sidewalk across the street there was a kid with a ball, who told me his mother always came to see him when he had a stomach ache. I had myself a stomach ache, but it didn't get me anything. Then I had convulsions, and that didn't help either. I even started to shit all over the apartment to get more attention. No soap. My mother didn't come and Madame Rosa called me an Arab asshole, for the first time—she'd never done it before because she wasn't French. I yelled that I wanted to see my mother, and for weeks I went on shitting all over the place to get even. In the end Madame Rosa said that if I went on like that it was the Public Welfare for me, and that scared me because the Public Welfare is the first thing they teach children. I kept on shitting for the principle of the thing, but it was no life. There were seven more kids boarding with Madame Rosa at the time, and they all started shitting for all they were worth, because kids are terrible conformists, and there was so much shit all over the place that I went unnoticed.

Madame Rosa was old and tired to begin with, and this kind of thing was very hard on her, because she'd already been persecuted for being Jewish. She dragged her two hundred and ten pounds up the six flights several times a day on her two poor legs, and when she came in and smelled all the shit she collapsed in her chair with her bundles and burst into tears, which is easy to understand. She said there were fifty million Frenchmen in France and if they'd all done what we did even the Germans couldn't have resisted, they'd have skedaddled, every last one of them. Madame Rosa had been in Germany during the war, but now she was back. She came in, she smelled the shit, and she started yelling: "This is Auschwitz! Auschwitz!" because she'd been deported to Auschwitz for the Jews. But when it comes to racism, she was okay. For instance, we had a little Moïse in the house, and she used to call him an Arab asshole, but never me. I didn't realize at the time what a sensitive soul she was in spite of her weight. I finally stopped shitting because I wasn't getting results and my mother didn't turn up, but I went on having cramps and convulsions for a long time, and even now it gives me a stomach ache some days. Later on I tried other ways of getting attention. I started swiping things from stores, a tomato or a melon, for instance, from out front. I always waited till somebody was looking, because I wanted to be seen. When the storekeeper came out and whacked me, I'd start to yell, but I was glad to have somebody taking an interest in me.

One time I swiped an egg from outside a butter and egg store. The storekeeper was a woman and she saw me. I liked to steal from places with a woman, because one thing I knew for sure was that my mother was a woman, it's inevitable. I took an egg and put it in my pocket. The woman came out and I waited for her to clout me and show some interest. But she squatted down beside me and patted me on the head. She even said:

"Aren't you the cutest thing!"

First I thought she was trying to get her egg back by playing on my heartstrings, and I held it tight at the bottom of my pocket. I only wanted her to punish me with a clout; that's what a mother does when she notices her kid. But she got up and went to the counter and gave me another egg. And then she kissed me. I had a moment of hope that I can't describe, because it's indescribable. All morning I waited outside that store. I don't know what I was waiting for. Once in a while the woman smiled at me, and I stood there holding my egg. I was six years old or thereabouts, and I thought it was for life, but it was only an egg. I went back home and I had a stomach ache all day. Madame Rosa was at the police station giving false testimony for Madame Lola. Madame Lola was a transvestite on the fifth floor and she worked her ass in the Bois de Boulogne. She'd been a boxing champion in Senegal before crossing over and she'd knocked out a sadistical customer who'd come to the wrong address, because how was he to know? Madame Rosa had testified that she'd spent that evening at the movies with Madame Lola and after the show they'd watched TV together. I'll be telling you more about Madame Lola, she was really somebody that wasn't like anybody else, and that's why I like her.

KIDS ARE VERY CONTAGIOUS. WHEN one starts up, the rest join in. There were seven of us at Madame Rosa's just then, including two day pupils, that Monsieur Moussa, the garbage man, delivered at 6 A.M. with the garbage truck, because his wife had died of something and wasn't there any more. Then in the afternoon he'd pick them up and take care of them. There was Moïse, who was even younger than me, and Banania, who was always laughing because he was born happy. Another was Michel. He'd had Vietnamese parents, and for the last year, ever since the money stopped coming, Madame Rosa had been saying she wasn't going to keep him another day. Madame Rosa was as good as gold, but she had her limits. A lot of those whores went to foreign countries where the pay was good and they'd leave their kids with Madame Rosa and never come back. It was just a case of toot-toot good-by. So this was a bunch of kids who weren't necessary and hadn't managed to get abortioned in time. Sometimes Madame Rosa placed them in families that felt lonely and needed the money, but it wasn't easy on account of the laws. When a woman has to hustle she loses her paternity rights, because it's prostitution. So she's afraid the kid

will be taken away from her and she hides him
with somebody she can trust. I couldn't tell you
how many little bastards I saw arriving at Madame
Rosa's, but most of them didn't stay for permanent like me. The ones who'd been there
longest after me were Moïse, Banania and the
Vietnamese, who was finally adopted by a
restaurant on the rue Monsieur le Prince. That
was a long time ago, and I wouldn't know him if I
met him on the street.

When I started yelling for my mother, Madame
Rosa told me to stop putting on airs. She even said
all Arabs were like that, you give them a finger
and they want the whole hand. Madame Rosa
wasn't really that way, it was only prejudice that
made her say such things, and I knew I was her
favorite. When I started yelling, the other kids
started yelling, so Madame Rosa had seven kids
on her hands, all bellowing for their mothers, and
it threw her into a regular fit of collective hysteria.
She tore her hair that she already didn't have, and
the tears ran down her cheeks with ingratitude.
She hid her face in her hands and cried and cried,
but kids are heartless at that age. There was even
plaster falling off the wall, not because Madame
Rosa was crying, only from wear and tear.

Madame Rosa had gray hair that was falling
too, because it had stopped caring very much one
way or the other. She was scared to death of going
bald, it's an awful thing for a woman who hasn't
got much else. She had more ass and bosom than
anybody you ever heard of, and when she looked
at herself in the glass, she always made a big smile,
like she was trying to vamp herself. On Sunday she

dolled up from top to toe, put on her red wig, and went to the Place Beaulieu, where she'd sit on a bench for several hours very elegantly. She put on makeup several times a day, but can you blame her! Under the wig and makeup her face wasn't so noticeable, and she always had flowers in the apartment to make her surroundings nicer.

When she calmed down, she dragged me to the can and said I was a ringleader and ringleaders always ended up in jail. She told me my mother saw everything I did and if I wanted to be reunited with her some day I should lead a clean honest life and keep away from juvenile delinquency. That can was very small and there wasn't room inside for all of Madame Rosa, because of her proportions. For somebody so alone it was amazing how much of her there was, and there in that can I think she must have felt more alone than ever.

When the money orders stopped coming for one of us, Madame Rosa didn't throw the culprit out. That's the way it was with little Bania. His father was unknown, so you couldn't put the blame on him; and his mother sent a little money every six months, sort of. Madame Rosa gave Bania a piece of her mind but he didn't care because he was only three years old and all smiles. I think Madame Rosa might have handed Bania over to the Welfare, but not his smile, and seeing as she couldn't have one without the other she had to keep them both. It was my job to take Bania to the African lodging houses on the rue Bisson to see black people. Madame Rosa thought that was very important.

"He's got to see black people. If he doesn't, he

won't want to mix with them later.''

So I took Banania next door. They were very nice to him because they'd left their families in Africa and one kid always reminds you of another. Madame Rosa had no idea whether Banania, whose real name was Touré, was a Malian, Senegalese, Guinean or something else. His mother had peddled her ass on the rue Saint-Denis before she went away to a house in Abidjan, which is in Africa, and in that business you never know who's knocked you up. Moïse was very irregular too, but there Madame Rosa was stuck, because between Jews the Public Welfare was out of the question. My case was different. A money order for three hundred francs arrived at the beginning of each month, which made me impregnable. I think Moïse had a mother and she was ashamed because the father was a goy; she came of a good family and her parents were in the dark. Moïse was blond with blue eyes, and, without the identificational nose; he looked so un-Jewish that it was a true confession.

My three hundred francs a month, cash on the line, inflicted a respectful attitude on Madame Rosa. I was going on ten and starting to have precocious trouble, because Arabs always get a hard-on before anyone else. So I knew I was solid gold to Madame Rosa and she'd think twice before crying wolf. That's what happened in the can when I was six. You'll say I'm mixing the years, but it's not true, and I'll explain when the time comes how I suddenly aged from one minute to the next.

"Listen to me, Momo, you're the oldest, so it's

up to you to set an example, so stop raising hell about your mother. You kids are lucky you don't know your mothers, because children your age still have sensibilities, and it's hard to believe what dyed-in-the-wool whores they are, sometimes I think I'm dreaming. Do you know what a whore is?''

"It's a person who peddles her ass."

"God only knows where you pick up such horrors, but there's a lot of truth in what you say."

"What about you, Madame Rosa? Did you peddle your ass when you were young and beautiful?"

She smiled. It made her happy to hear she'd been young and beautiful.

"You're a good little boy, Momo. But behave yourself. Help me. I'm old and sick. I've had nothing but trouble since I got out of Auschwitz."

She was so sad you didn't even notice she was ugly. I threw my arms around her neck and kissed her. The people on our street said she was a woman without a heart, and it's true she had no one to look after her. She'd managed without a heart for sixty-five years and there were times when you couldn't help forgiving her.

She cried so hard I had to piss.

"Excuse me, Madame Rosa, I've got to piss."

Afterwards I said:

"All right, Madame Rosa, I know I can't have my mother, it can't be done, but couldn't we have a dog instead?"

"What? What! You think we have room for a dog? How am I going to feed it? Who's going to send *him* money orders?''

But she didn't say anything when I stole a little gray poodle from the kennel on the rue Calefeutre and brought him home. I went into the kennel and asked if I could pet the poodle, and the owner gave me the dog when I looked at her the way I know how. I took him, I petted him, and I lit out like an arrow. If there's one thing I'm good at, it's running. You can't get through life without it.

I REALLY WENT OVERBOARD FOR THAT dog. I loved him more than anyone's business. So did the other kids, except maybe Banania, who didn't give a damn about him, because he was already happy in the first place, for no reason at all—I've never seen a black man happy for any reason. I held that dog in my arms wherever I went, but I couldn't find a name for him. Every time Tarzan or Zorro came into my head, I felt there had to be a name somewhere that hadn't found a taker and was just waiting. In the end I chose Super, but only on consignment, reserving the right to change if I dug up something better. I had a lot of surplus stored up inside me, and I gave it all to Super. I don't know what I'd have done without that dog, it was really urgent. I'd probably have ended up in jail. When I took him out walking, I felt important, because I was all he had in the world. I loved him so much that I finally gave him away. I was nine by then, or thereabouts, and at that age you begin to think, except maybe if you're happy. Besides, between you and me, without wanting to hurt anybody's feelings, it was gloomy at Madame Rosa's, even when you were used to it. So when Super started growing on me, emotionally speaking, I decided to

give him a better life. I'd have done the same for
myself if I'd been able. And don't forget: Super
wasn't anything the cat dragged in; he was a
genuine poodle. Well, this lady saw him and said:
"My, what a pretty little dog!" And then she
asked if he was mine and for sale. I wasn't dressed
very fancy and I don't look French. She could see
that me and Super were two different breeds.

I sold him to her for five hundred francs, and he
was really getting a good bargain. I asked this lady
for five hundred francs because I wanted to be
sure she could afford the upkeep. I was in luck;
she even had a car with a driver, and before I knew
it she stowed Super in the car, in case I had parents
and they started yelling. And now I'm going to tell
you something, because you won't believe me. I
took her five hundred francs and threw them
down the sewer. Then I sat down on the sidewalk
and bawled like a baby with my fists in my eyes,
but I was happy. There was no security at
Madame Rosa's, we were all hanging by a thread,
with no money and Madame Rosa sick and the
Public Welfare at our throats. That was no life for
a dog.

When I went home and told I'd sold Super for
five hundred francs and thrown the money down
the sewer, Madame Rosa was scared to death. She
stared at me and ran to her room and double-
locked the door. After that she always locked herself in at night, for fear I'd cut her throat again.
The other kids screamed and yelled when they
heard about it, but they didn't really care about
Super, they were only pretending.

There was a big bunch of us at the time, seven

or eight. One of them was Salima. Her mother had managed to save her when the neighbors reported her as a whore and the Public Welfare raided her for parental unfitness. She interrupted her customer in the middle, went to the kitchen, where she'd left Salima, got her out through the window and hid her all night in a garbage can. In the morning she brought the kid to Madame Rosa, smelling of garbage in a state of hysteria. Another transient was Antoine. He was a real French kid, the only native we'd ever had, and we examined him carefully to see how he was built. But he was only two, so there wasn't much to see. I don't remember who else was there, because they were always changing, with mothers coming and taking their kids back and others bringing new ones. Madame Rosa said that whores didn't get enough moral support, because a lot of the pimps aren't as conscientious as they used to be. They need their kids to give them something to live for. They'd come around when they had a moment to spare or when they'd caught some disease and they thought they'd take advantage of the break by going to the country with their kid. I've never understood why they don't let registered whores bring up their kids. Nobody bothers the other kind, do they? Madame Rosa thought it was because fucking is so important in France, much more than anywhere else, you wouldn't believe the proportions it assumes if you hadn't seen it with your own eyes. Madame Rosa used to say that next to Louis XIV fucking was the biggest thing in France, which is why prostitutes, as they're sometimes called, are

persecuted, because respectable women want it all
to themselves. I've seen mothers crying at
Madame Rosa's place because they'd been reported to the police for having a kid in their line of
work and they were half dead with fear. Madame
Rosa told them not to worry; she said she knew a
police inspector who protected her because he'd
been a whore's kid himself, in addition to a Jew
who made her false papers that were so authentic
nobody could tell the difference. I never saw that
Jew, because Madame Rosa kept him hidden.
They'd known each other at the home for Jews in
Germany. They hadn't been exterminated by
mistake and they'd sworn not to let it happen
again. This Jew was tucked away in some French
neighborhood, where he made false papers like
mad, and thanks to him Madame Rosa could
always prove she was somebody else. Even the
Israelis, she used to say, couldn't get anything on
her. Of course her mind was never a hundred per
cent at rest, because for that you've got to be
dead. Life is always a panic.

So, as I was telling you, the kids yelled for
several hours when I gave Super away for the sake
of his future, which wouldn't have been secure at
Madame Rosa's, all except Banania, who was perfectly happy. Take it from me, that little son of a
bitch was a case, four years old and still happy.

The first thing Madame Rosa did next day was
to drag me to Dr. Katz's to see if I was deranged.
Madame Rosa wanted him to give me a blood test,
because all Arabs are syphilitic, but Dr. Katz got
so mad his beard jiggled, because I forgot to tell

you he had a beard. He bawled Madama Rosa out good and proper and accused her of bandying Orléans rumors.*

No disappearance was reported to the police. The press and radio spoke of the rumor but never recorded any incident that might have justified it. Nevertheless the rumor spread all over France and persisted for over a month. Orléans rumors were when some Jews in the ready-to-wear business in Orléans didn't drug certain white girls and didn't ship them off to the white slave trade. Everybody was down on them because the Jews are always getting publicity for nothing.

Madame Rosa was still shaken.

"Now tell me exactly what happened."

"He took five hundred francs and threw them down the sewer."

"Was that his first fit of violence?"

Madame Rosa didn't answer; she just looked at me, and I felt very sad. I'm philosophical and I've never liked to make people unhappy. Behind Dr. Katz there was a sailboat on a mantelpiece with snow-white wings. I was so miserable I wanted to go away, far far away, and I started to make it fly, I went on board and crossed the oceans with a steady hand. I think it was on Dr. Katz's sailboat that I sailed away for the first time. Up until then I can't really say I was a child. Even now, when I want, I can board Dr. Katz's sailboat and sail

*In May 1969 a rumor arose in Orléans, a city of 170,000 inhabitants, only seventy miles from Paris, that several women had disappeared from the dressing rooms of six Jewish clothing shops, that the shopkeepers had drugged them and shipped them off to the white slave market.

away all by myself. I never told anyone about it. When I was with somebody, I always pretended to be right there on dry land.

"Doctor, I beg you to give this child a thorough examination. You tell me to avoid emotion on account of my heart, and what does this child do? He sells what he loves best in all the world and throws five hundred francs down the sewer. Even in Auschwitz nobody did that."

Dr. Katz was well known to all the Jews and Arabs in the neighborhood for his Christian charity. He treated them from morning to night and then some. I've kept a pleasant memory of him, his office was the only place where anybody talked to me and examined me as if I were important. A lot of times I went there alone, not because I was sick, just to sit in the waiting room. I'd stay quite a while. He knew I had no business there and I was using up a chair when there was so much misery in the world, but he always gave me a friendly smile and never got angry. I often thought when I looked at Dr. Katz that if somebody had offered me a father it's him I'd have chosen.

"He loved that dog more than anyone's business, he held him in his arms even when he went to bed. And what does he do? He sells him and throws the money away. The child isn't normal. There must have been sudden madness in his family."

"I can assure you that nothing will happen, absolutely nothing, Madame Rosa."

I began to cry. I knew nothing would happen, but it was the first time I'd heard anyone say so in so many words.

"There's nothing to cry about, my little Mohammed. But go ahead and cry if it makes you feel better. Does he cry much?"

"Never," said Madame Rosa. "He never cries, and God knows I suffer."

"Well," said the doctor. "You see he's better already. His crying is a sign of normal development. You were right to bring him, Madame Rosa. For yourself I'll prescribe tranquilizers. Your trouble is anxiety, that's all."

"Anyone who takes care of children had better be anxious, or they'll turn into thugs."

We walked home hand in hand. Madame Rosa likes to be seen in company. She always takes a long time dressing before she goes out because she used to be a woman and hasn't entirely gotten over it. She puts on a lot of paint but it doesn't hide her age any more. She has a face like an old Jewish frog with glasses and asthma. When she climbs the stairs with her shopping, she has to stop all the time. She says that one of these days she'll drop dead in the middle, as if it were so important to get to the top of all six flights.

WHEN WE GOT BACK, MONSIEUR N'DA Amédée, the well-known pimp, sometimes known as a procurer, was there. If you've been around that neighborhood, you know it's full of natives, who all come from Africa as the word indicates. They've got several lodging houses, some people call them tenements, lacking the barest necessities, such as hygiene and central heating. Some of those black lodging houses have as many as a hundred and twenty inmates, with eight to a room and only one can, at the foot of the stairs, so they go wherever they can, because those things won't wait. Before my time there were shantytowns, but the government cleared them away because they made a bad impression. Madame Rosa once told me about a lodging house where they suffocated a whole crowd of Senegalese with coal stoves by putting them in a room with the windows closed and next morning they were dead, asphyxiated by the poisonous influences that came out of the stove while they were sleeping the sleep of the just. I used to go and see them on the rue Bisson next door, and they were always nice to me. Most of them were Moslems like me, but that wasn't the reason. I think it gave them pleasure to see a nine-year-old kid who was too young to have any ideas.

Grownups always have ideas. For instance, they think all black people look alike, and it's not true.

Madame Sambor, who cooked for them, didn't look the least bit like Monsieur Dia once you were used to the darkness. Monsieur Dia was no joke. He had eyes that must have been made to scare people with. He was always reading. Besides, he had a razor this long, and when you pressed a catch the blade didn't fold. He used it to shave with, but never mind. There were fifty in the house and they were all at his beck and call. When he wasn't reading, he was doing gymnastics on the floor because he wanted to be stronger than anyone else. He was all muscle already, but that wasn't good enough for him. I couldn't see what a big bruiser like him needed all that body building for. I never asked him, but my suspicion is that he didn't feel strong enough for all the things he wanted to do. It's the same with me. Sometimes I want to be strong so bad I think I'm going to bust. I dream of being a cop afraid of neither man nor beast. I used to hang around for hours outside the police station on the rue Deudon, though I knew there was no hope; they won't take a nine-year-old, because at that age you're a minority. I dreamed of being a cop because the common pavement pounders were the biggest and strongest, I'd never heard of sergeants and inspectors. It wasn't until much later that I found out there were even higher things to dream of, but I never went as high as the Prefect of Police; my imagination wasn't up to it. I must have been, say, eight, nine or ten, and I was scared pink of waking up all alone in the world. The more trouble

Madame Rosa had climbing the stairs and the longer she sat down afterwards, the smaller and scareder I felt.

Another thing that bugged me was the question of my date, especially when they said I was too young for my age and sent me home from school. It really didn't matter, because the certificate proving I'd been born was false. As I've told you, Madame Rosa had a whole collection of them; she could even prove she hadn't been Jewish for several generations, if the police started searching the house for her. She'd taken every possible precaution since the French police, that supplied the Germans with victims, had grabbed her by surprise and shut her up in a Velodrome for Jews. Later they sent her to a home for Jews in Germany where they burned them. She was always afraid, not like everybody else, but even more.

One night I heard her yelling in her sleep. It woke me up and I saw her getting out of bed. There were two rooms, and she kept one of them all for herself except when we were overcrowded, then Moïse and I slept with her. That's the way it was that night, but Moïse wasn't with us, some Jewish family without children was interested in him and they'd taken him home for observation to see if he was worth adopting. He was trying so hard to make a good impression that he was always knocked out when he got back. They had a kosher grocery store on the rue Tienné.

So Madame Rosa woke me up with her yelling. She switched on the light. Her head was trembling and her eyes looked like she was seeing something. She got up out of bed and put on her wrapper and took a key that was hidden under the cupboard. When she bends down, her ass is even bigger than usual.

She went to the stairs and started down. I was scared to stay alone, so I followed her.

On her way down the stairs, Madame Rosa was in the dark half the time, because the minute-light in our house is very short for economic reasons; the landlord's a bastard. Once when the darkness fell, I pressed the light button like a dope, and Madame Rosa, who was one flight lower, let out a scream, because she thought it was a human presence. She looked up, she looked down, and then she started moving again. So did I, but I stopped fiddling with the minute-light; you see, we had scared each other. I had no idea what was going on, even less than usual, and that always makes it scarier. My knees were chattering and it was spooky to see that woman going down the stairs as crafty as a Sioux, as if the whole place were full of enemies and then some.

When she got to the bottom, Madame Rosa didn't go out in the street. She turned left and headed for the cellar stairs, where there isn't any light and it's dark even in the summer. She'd forbidden us to go there because that's where they always strangle children. When Madame Rosa took those stairs, I thought this is the end, she's gone off her rocker. I was thinking of running and waking up Dr. Katz. But by that time I was so scared I thought I'd better stay right there and not move. I was sure that if I moved, the monsters would start howling and jump me from all sides, instead of staying hidden like they'd done ever since I was born.

Then I saw a ray of light. It came from the cellar and I felt better after that. Monsters don't usually turn on the light, they feel more at home in the dark.

I went to the bottom of the stairs and followed a corridor that smelled of piss, etcetera, because there was only one can for a hundred people in the black lodging house next door, and they did their business wherever they could. The cellar was divided into different compartments and one of the doors was open. That's where Madame Rosa had gone and the light came from. I looked in.

In the middle of the room there was a rickety red armchair; it was all filthy and stove-in, and Madame Rosa was sitting in it. The walls were made of stones that stuck out like teeth and looked as if they were laughing. A candlestick with Jewish branches was perched on top of a washstand and one of the candles was lit. And then, to my amazement, I saw a bed; it was a wreck, fit for the junkheap, but it had a mattress, blankets and pillows. I also saw some sacks of potatoes, a cook stove, some kerosene cans and a carton of sardines. I was too flabbergasted to be scared any more, except that my ass was bare and I was beginning to feel cold.

Madame Rosa sat in her ramshackle armchair, beaming from every pore. The look on her face was smug, I'd almost say triumphant, like she'd done something awfully clever. After a while she got up. There was a broom in one corner and she started sweeping the cellar. It was a dumb thing to do because it raised dust and nothing was worse than dust for her asthma. In half a second she was wheezing and choking, but she went on sweeping, because there was no one to tell her but me, nobody gave a damn. I know she was paid to take care of me and the only thing we had in common was that we were both alone in the world with nothing and nobody, but there was nothing worse than dust for her asthma. When she was through, she put the broom down and tried to blow out the candle, but in spite of her size she didn't have the wind. She wet her fingers with her tongue and put the candle out that way. Then I beat it, because I knew she'd finished and was going back up.

Naturally I didn't get it, but there were plenty of things I didn't get. Why in God's name would it give her a kick to go down six flights of stairs and then some in the middle of the night, just to sit in her cellar compartment looking clever?

When she came back up again, she wasn't afraid any more, and neither was I, because it's contagious. We slept the sleep of the just side by side. But I've thought about it, and I think Monsieur Hamil is mistaken when he says that. I'd say the unjust were the soundest sleepers, because they don't give a damn; it's the just that lie awake, worrying about every little thing, they wouldn't be just if they didn't. Monsieur Hamil always uses far-out expressions, like "trust my long experience" or "as I had the honor of telling you" and that kind of thing; I like them because they remind me of him. He taught me to write "the language of my ancestors" (he always said "ancestors" because he didn't think my parents were mentionable) and to read the Koran because Madame Rosa said it was good for Arabs. When I asked her how she knew my name was Mohammed and I was a good Moslem, when I had no father or mother or document to prove it, she looked unhappy and said she'd explain it all some day when I was big and strong, but she didn't want to give me a fatal shock when I still had feelings. She always said the first thing you had to watch out for in children was feelings. I suppose so, but it was all one to me that my mother peddled her ass for a living, and if I'd known her I'd have loved her and been a good pimp to her, like Monsieur N'Da Amédée, whom I shall have the honor of telling you about. I was mighty glad to have Madame Rosa, but if I'd been offered someone better and more my own, I wouldn't have said no, hell no! I could have looked after Madame Rosa even if I'd had a real mother to look after. Monsieur N'Da Amédée gives his protection to several women at once.

If Madame Rosa knew I was Mohammed and a Moslem, it meant I came from some place. So I kept asking where she was and why she didn't come and see me. But Madame Rosa always started crying and said I had no gratitude and didn't love her and wanted somebody else. So I dropped the subject. All right, I know there's always a mystery when a kid gets born because a women who hustles for a living hasn't been able to stop it in time with hygiene. But in that case, how come Madame Rosa was so dead sure I was Mohammed and a Moslem? She couldn't have made it up just to please me. I asked Monsieur Hamil one time when he was telling me the life of Sidi Abderrahman, who was the patron saint of Algiers.

Monsieur Hamil comes from Algiers, where he went on a pilgrimage to Mecca thirty years ago. So naturally Sidi Abderrahman of Algiers is his favorite saint, because the shirt is always closest to the skin, as he says. But he also has a carpet with a picture of another compatriot, Sidi Ouali Dada, sitting on a prayer rug that's being towed by fishes. Fishes pulling a carpet through the air doesn't seem to make much sense, but religion is like that.

"Monsieur Hamil, how come I'm known as Mohammed and a Moslem when I've got nothing to prove it?"

Monsieur Hamil always raises one hand when he wants to say God's will be done.

"Madame Rosa took you in when you were very little and she doesn't keep a birth register. She has seen a great many children come and go since then, my little Mohammed. She is bound by professional secrecy, because some of the ladies insist on discretion. She put you down as Mohammed, therefore a Moslem, and your father was never heard from after that. The only sign of life he ever gave Madame Rosa was you. And you are a fine child. Perhaps your father was killed in the Algerian War. A fine thing, a splendid thing! A hero of independence!"

"Monsieur Hamil, I'd rather have a father than not have a hero. Why couldn't he just have been a good pimp and taken care of my mother?"

"You mustn't talk like that, my little Mohammed. Don't forget the Yugoslavs and the Corsicans. Why should we Arabs get blamed for everything? It's hard to raise a child in this neighborhood."

All the same I had a feeling that Monsieur Hamil knew something he wasn't letting on. He was a fine man and if he hadn't sold carpets from door to door all his life, he'd have been very famous, I wouldn't be surprised to see him sitting on a flying carpet pulled by fishes, like that Algerian saint, Sidi Ouali Dada.

"And why did they send me home from school, Monsieur Hamil? Madame Rosa said it was because I was too young for my age, then the next time I was too old for my age, and the third time my age wasn't right for me, so she dragged me to see Dr. Katz, and he told her maybe I'd grow up to be somebody very special, a great poet, for instance."

Monsieur Hamil seemed very sad. That was because of his eyes. It's always in the eyes that people are the saddest.

"You're a very sensitive child, my little Mohammed. That makes you a little different from the others . . ."

He smiled.

"Sensitive people don't grow on trees nowadays."

He said that in Arabic and it doesn't sound as good in French.

"Was my father a big bandit, Monsieur Hamil? Is that why everybody's afraid of even mentioning him?"

"Oh no, Mohammed, certainly not. I've never heard anything of the kind."

"Then what have you heard, Monsieur Hamil?"

He lowered his eyes and sighed.

"Nothing."

"Nothing?"

"Nothing."

With me it was always the same thing. Nothing.

The lesson was over and Monsieur Hamil began talking about Nice, which is my favorite story. When he talks about clowns dancing in the streets and happy giants sitting on floats, I feel at home. I also like the mimosa forests down there and the palm trees, and they've got snow-white birds that are so enthusiastic they flap their wings the way other people would clap their hands. One day I persuaded Moïse and some other kid with a different name to hike down to Nice with me and live in the mimosa forest on the game we bagged. We started out one morning and got as far as the Place Pigalle, but then we were scared because it was far from home and we went back. Madame Rosa thought she was going out of her mind, but she always says that to express herself.

So, as I've had the honor, when Madame Rosa and I got back after seeing Dr. Katz, Monsieur N'Da Amédée was there. You never saw such a well-dressed man. He was the biggest black pimp and procurer in all Paris, and he came to see us for Madame Rosa to write letters to his family, because he didn't want anybody else to know he couldn't write. He was wearing a pink silk suit that he let me touch with a pink hat and a pink shirt. His tie was pink too and that outfit made him look really unusual. He came from Niger, which is one of the numerous countries they've got in Africa, and he made himself, as he kept telling us. "I'm a self-made man," he'd say with his suit and diamond rings. He had one on each finger and when he was murdered in the Seine they cut off his fingers for the rings, because it was a settling of accounts. I'm telling you this right now so as not to upset you later on. In his lifetime he owned the best eighty feet of sidewalk in Pigalle and he had his nails manicured, which were pink too. Oh, I forget, he was also wearing a vest. He kept touching his moustache with his fingertips, very gently, like he wanted to be nice to it. He always brought Madame Rosa a little something sweet. She'd have preferred perfume, because she was afraid of getting even fatter. I never saw her smelling bad until much later. So perfume was the right kind of present for Madame Rosa; she had bottles and bottles of it, but I could never understand why she put it mostly behind her ears, like parsley on a calf's head. This black man I've been telling you about, this Monsieur N'Da Amédée, was really illiterate, because success had come too late to go to school. I'm not going to write history all over again, but I can tell you that the black people have suffered an awful lot, and we should try and understand them when we can. That's why Monsieur N'Da Amédée got Madame Rosa to write the letters he sent his parents in Niger, because, you see, he knew their name. They'd had a terrible time with racism down there, but then came the revolution, which ushered in a régime, and after that they were all right. I haven't had any trouble with racism myself, so I don't know what I should look forward to. Well, I suppose the black people have other faults.

Monsieur N'Da Amédée would sit on the bed where we slept when there were only three or four of us; when there were more we slept with Madame Rosa. Or he'd put one foot on the bed and stand on the other and tell Madame Rosa what to say to his parents in writing. While he was talking, Monsieur N'Da Amédée used to gesticulate and work himself into a lather, not because he was angry, but because he had many more things to say to his parents than he could express with his low-class resources. It always began with Dear and Revered Father, and then he'd get into a temper because he was bursting with marvelous things that weighed on his heart because he couldn't get them off his chest. If speech is silver, as they say, he'd have needed gold and diamonds for every word. Madame Rosa made up letters saying he was taking illiteracy courses to make him a director of public works, and when he graduated he'd come back and build dams and be a benefactor to his country. When she read him what she had written, he beamed all over. She also had him building bridges and roads and everything else they needed. It gave her pleasure to see how happy it made Monsieur N'Da Amédée to hear all the things he did in his letters, and he always put money in the envelope to make them even truer. He and his pink suit from the Champs-Élysées or maybe even fancier were in seventh heaven, and when he'd gone Madame Rosa told me that while he was listening he had the eyes of a true believer. She said the blacks of Africa, because they've got them in other countries too, are the world's champion believers. True believers are people who believe in God, like Monsieur Hamil, who was always talking about God and telling me you've got to learn those things when you're young and capable of believing anything.

Monsieur N'Da Amédée had a diamond in his tie that sparkled. Madame Rosa said it was a real diamond and not a fake as one might think, because you can never be too careful. Madame Rosa's maternal grandfather was in the diamond business and she had inherited some of his experience. The diamond was just under Monsieur N'Da Amédée's face, which sparkled too, but not for the same reasons. Madame Rosa never remembered what she'd put in the last letter to his parents in Africa, but it didn't matter; she used to say that the more people haven't got the more they're willing to believe. Anyway, Monsieur N'Da Amédée wasn't hard to please; he didn't care what she wrote as long as it made his parents happy. Sometimes he even forgot his parents and talked to himself about all the things he had done and was planning to do. I'd never known anybody who could talk about himself like that, as if nothing was impossible. He'd shout that everybody respected him and that he was the king. "That's right!" he'd yell, "I'm the king!" And Madame Rosa would put it in writing, with the bridges and dams, the whole public works. When he'd gone, she'd say Monsieur N'Da Amédée was completely *meshugga,* which means nuts in Yiddish, but that he was a dangerous nut and it was best to humor him if you knew what was good for you. It seems he'd already killed a few people, but that was between blacks and they had no identity, because they're not French like the American blacks and the police only bother about people who exist. One day, later on, he got into hostilities with some Algerians and Corsicans and she had to write his parents the kind of letter that's no joy to anyone. You mustn't go thinking that pimps don't have their problems same as everyone else.

Monsieur N'Da Amédée always came around with two bodyguards, because he wasn't very safe and he needed protection. Those bodyguards had such ugly mugs, they were so terrifying to look at, you'd have given them the shirt off your back in a big hurry. One of them had been a boxer and his face had taken so much punishment that everything was out of place, one eye was in too deep, the nose was crushed, some of his eyebrows had been torn off when the referee stopped the fight, and there was something wrong with the other eye too, as if the punch that had pushed the first eye in had pushed this one out. But you've never seen such fists and arms. Madame Rosa used to tell me that you grow faster if you dream a lot. This Monsieur Boro's fists were so enormous they must have dreamed ever since they were born.

The face of the other bodyguard was still intact, but more's the pity. I don't like people with faces that are always changing, that shift in all directions and never look the same twice in a row. You wouldn't have trusted that man around the corner, I guess he had something to hide, who hasn't, but that bodyguard, I'm telling you, looked so false it made your hair stand on end just to wonder what he could be dreaming up. See what I mean? In addition he was always smiling at me, and it's not true that black people put children in their sandwiches. That's a lot of Orléans rumors, but I always had a feeling that I made his mouth water and after all they were cannibals in Africa, you've got to give them credit. When I went anywhere near him, he'd grab me and put me on his lap and tell me he had a little boy my age and he'd given him a cowboy outfit like I'd always wanted. A real stinker. Maybe there was some good in him like everybody else if you look hard, but he scared the shit out of me with those eyes of his that never pointed the same way twice in succession. He must have known it too, because he was such a two-face that one time he even brought me some pistachio nuts. Pistachio nuts don't mean a thing, they only cost a franc, tax and service included. If he thought he could make friends with that, he was barking up the wrong tree. I'm telling you all this because it shows why I had another fit of violence, under circumstances beyond my control.

Monsieur N'Da Amédée always came to dictate on Sunday. Women don't hustle that day, it's the truce of God, so one or two of them would always come around to take their kids to the park for a breath of air or treat them to lunch. I can assure you that some whores are the best of mothers, because it's a change from their customers and besides a kid gives them a future. Of course there are some that drop out of sight and you never hear from them again, but that doesn't mean they're not dead or haven't got some other excuse. Sometimes they didn't bring their kids back until noon the next day, so's to keep them as long as possible before going back to the daily grind. So that day only the permanent kids were home, which was mostly me and Banania, who hadn't paid a sou since last year but that didn't faze him in the least, you'd have thought he owned the place. Moïse was there too, but by then he was pending with a Jewish family that only wanted to make sure he didn't have anything hereditary, as I've had the honor, because that's the first thing you've got to think of when you start loving a kid if you don't want trouble later on. Dr. Katz had given him a certificate, but those people wanted to be sure before they took the plunge. Banania was even happier than usual, he's just discovered his pecker, and that was his first experience in life. I was learning words I couldn't make heads or tails of, but Monsieur Hamil had written them out by hand and it didn't matter. I can still recite them for you, he'd be pleased if he knew it: *elli habb allāh lā ibri ghirhu subhān ad-daim lā iazul* . . . Which means, He who loves God desires nothing beside Him . . . Personally, I desired a good deal more, but Monsieur Hamil was making me learn my religion because even if I stayed in France until death do us part, like Monsieur Hamil himself, he wanted me to remember that I had a country of my own, which is better than nothing. My country must have been Algeria or Morocco or some such place. Even if I didn't figure in anybody's documents, Madame Rosa was sure of that, she wasn't bringing me up to be an Arab for the fun of it. Anyway, she said that as far as she was concerned those things didn't matter, all men were equal when steeped in misery and shit, and if the Jews and the Arabs clobber each other it's because whatever you may say to the contrary the Jews and the Arabs are no different from anybody else, which is the whole principle of brotherhood, except maybe the Germans, who are even more so. I forgot to tell you that Madame Rosa kept a big picture of Monsieur Hitler under her bed and when she was so unhappy she couldn't bear it she took it out and gazed at it, and in half a second she felt better because that was one less thing to worry about.

Jewish or not, Madame Rosa was a very good woman. I won't deny it, she only gave us the cheapest stuff to eat, and she really got me down with the Ramadan business. From her point of view, as you can well imagine, twenty days of fasting were manna from heaven, and you should have seen the gloating look on her face when Ramadan came around and I had to go without my share of her gefillte fish. She respected the beliefs of others, but I'd seen her eating ham, the stinker. When I told her she wasn't allowed, she just laughed. There was nothing I could do to stop her from taking advantage of Ramadan, and I had to steal stuff from grocery stores in a neighborhood where I wasn't known as an Arab.

So it was Sunday at Madame Rosa's. Madame Rosa had spent the morning crying, she had her days when she cried the whole time for no reason. I never pestered her when she was crying because those were her happiest moments. Oh yes, now I remember, she'd given the little Viet a spanking that morning because he always hid under the bed when the doorbell rang. He'd changed families twenty times in three years and he was fed up. I don't know what's become of him, but I'll go and see one of these days. To tell you the truth, none of us liked the doorbell very much, because we were always afraid of being raided by the Public Welfare. Madame Rosa had all the false papers she wanted, she'd fixed it up with a Jewish friend who'd worked day and night forging papers for the future ever since he'd come back alive. I don't remember if I told you, but she was also protected by a police inspector she had brought up while his mother was claiming to be a hairdresser in the provinces. But there are always envious tongues,

and Madame Rosa was afraid of being denounced, partly because one time she'd been
woken up at six o'clock in the morning by
somebody ringing the bell at the crack of dawn,
and they'd taken her to a Velodrome and from
there to a home for Jews in Germany. So then
Monsieur N'Da Amédée turned up with his two
bodyguards to dictate a letter, including the one
who looked like such a two-face that nobody
could stand him. I don't know why I'd taken such
a dislike to him, but I think it was because I was
nine or ten years old, maybe more, and I already
needed somebody to hate like other people.

Monsieur N'Da Amédée had put one foot on
the bed and he was holding a big cigar that was
shedding ashes in all directions regardless of the
expense. The first thing he told his parents was
that he'd soon be going back to Niger to become a
public benefactor. At present I think he believed it
himself. I've often noticed that people end up
believing what they say. They can't live without it.
I'm not saying that to sound like a philosopher, I
really believe it.

I forgot to tell you that this police inspector
with the whore for a mother had learned all and
forgiven all. He even came to see Madame Rosa
now and then and gave her a big kiss on condition
that she keep her trap shut. That's what Monsieur
Hamil means when he says that all's well that ends
well. I'm telling you this to throw in a laugh.

While Monsieur N'Da Amédée was talking, his
left-hand bodyguard was sitting in an armchair
shining his nails and the other wasn't paying attention. I wanted to go and piss, but on my way

out the second bodyguard, the one I've told you
about, grabbed me and put me on his lap. He
looked at me, smiled, tilted his head back and
spoke as follows:

"Momo, my boy, you remind me of my son.
He's in Nice by the seashore with his mummy, and
they're coming back tomorrow. It's the little
fellow's birthday tomorrow, that's the day he was
born, and he's getting a bicycle. You can come
and play with him any time you please."

I don't know what got into me, but I hadn't had
a father or mother for years, not to mention a
bicycle, and now this bastard starts bugging me.
See what I mean? Okay, *insh'Allah,* but it's not
true, I only say that because I'm a good Moslem.
That stirred me up and I broke out in a fit of
violence, something terrible. This fit came from
inside me and those are the worst. When they
come from outside, like somebody kicking you in
the ass, you can run away. From inside you're
helpless. When the violence grabs hold of me, I
want to get out and never come back. It's like I
had somebody living inside me. I howl and I yell, I
throw myself on the ground, I bash my head to get
out, but it can't be done, there's no legs, you've
got no legs inside you. It does me good to talk
about it, that lets some part of it out. See what I
mean?

Well, when I was exhausted and they'd all left,
Madame Rosa dragged me to see Dr. Katz. She
was scared out of her wits. She told him I had all
the hereditary symptoms and what was to stop me
from picking up a knife and stabbing her in her
sleep? I don't know why Madame Rosa was

always afraid of being killed in her sleep, as if that would have woken her up. Dr. Katz got good and mad. He said I was as gentle as a lamb and she ought to be ashamed. He gave her some tranquilizers he had in his drawer and we went home hand in hand. I could feel she was sorry she'd accused me unjustly. But you've got to understand her, because life was all she had left. People seem to care more about life than anything else, which is funny when you think of all the wonderful things there are in this world.

WHEN WE GOT HOME, SHE STUFFED herself full of tranquilizers and spent the evening looking at the air with a happy smile because she didn't feel anything. She never gave me any. That woman was the cream of the crop, and I can give you an illustration right now. Take Madame Sophie, who keeps another illegal nursery on the rue Surcouf, or the one they call the Comtesse because her name is the widow Comte. Well, sometimes they've got as many as ten day boarders, and the first thing they do is stuff them full of tranquilizers. Madame Rosa heard it from a reliable source, a Portuguese African woman who hustled not far from the Bastille and took her kid away from the Comtesse in such a state of stupor that he kept falling down because he couldn't stand up. Every time you stood him on his feet he'd fall down again, and you could play with him like that for hours. With Madame Rosa it was just the opposite. When we got jumpy, or we had day boarders that were seriously disturbed—it happens—she was the one that took the tranquilizers. Those days we could yell or beat each other up to our heart's content, it didn't make a dent in her. It was up to me to keep order on those days, and I liked that because it made me feel superior. Madame Rosa would be sitting in an armchair in the middle of the room, with a woolen frog on her belly and a hot water bottle inside. She'd tilt her head just a little and look at us with a pleasant smile, and now and then she'd wave at us, like we were a passing train. She was dead to the world on those tranquilized days of hers, and I'd be in command to stop them from setting fire to the curtains, which are the first things you set fire to when you're young.

The only thing that could upset Madame Rosa when she was tranquilized was the doorbell. She was scared pink of the Germans. It's an old story, it was in all the papers, so I won't go into details, but Madame Rosa never got over it. Sometimes she thought it was still going on, especially in the middle of the night. She was the kind of person who lived on her memories. Naturally it's idiotic in this day and age, when all that stuff is dead and buried, but the Jews are very obstinate, especially when they've been exterminated; those are the ones who come back the most. She often talked to me about the Nazis and the SS, and I'm kind of sorry I was born too late to know the Nazis and the SS and everything they did, because then at least I'd have known why and now I don't.

Madame Rosa's fear of the doorbell was really comical. The best time for it was very early in the morning, when the daylight is still coming on tiptoes. The Germans get up early and the small hours of the morning are their favorite time of day. One of us kids would get up and go out in the hallway and push the bell. A loud ring, meaning open quick or else. Did we laugh! You should

Emile Ajar

have been there. Madame Rosa must have weighed about two hundred and twenty at the time. She'd jump out of bed like a madwoman and be halfway ~~down~~ the stairs before she stopped. We'd all be in bed, pretending to be asleep. When she saw it wasn't the Nazis, she'd get roaring mad and call us a lot of sons of bitches, which she never did without good reason. She'd stand there awhile in a daze with the curlers in her last remaining hair. At first she'd think she'd been dreaming and the bell hadn't rung at all and the sound hadn't come from outside. But nearly every time one of us kids would burst out laughing, and when she realized she'd been a victim she'd fly into a rage or start crying.

- In my opinion, Jews are people like everyone else, but that's no reason to be down on them.

Sometimes we didn't even have to get up and ring the bell. Madame Rosa did it all by herself. Suddenly something would wake her, she'd sit up and listen, and then she'd jump out of bed, giving us a view of her ass that was even bigger than I can describe, throw on her favorite purple shawl, and run out the door. She didn't even look to see if anyone was there, because the ringing kept on inside her, that's where it's worst. Sometimes she'd run only a few steps or one floor down, and sometimes she'd go as far as the cellar, like the first time that I've had the honor. At first I thought she'd hidden a treasure in the cellar and been woken by fear of thieves. I've always dreamed of having a treasure hidden in some good place that I could discover any time I needed it. I think a treasure is about the best thing you can

44

have, if it's really yours and you can keep it safe. I'd ferreted out the place where Madame Rosa hid the key to the cellar, and one time I went down and looked. I didn't find a thing. Furniture, a chamber pot, sardines, candles, the kind of stuff you'd need if you had a secret lodger. I lit a candle and looked around, but all I could see was those walls with stones that showed their teeth. Then I heard a sound that made me jump sky-high, but it was only Madame Rosa. She was standing in the doorway looking at me. It wasn't an angry look, more on the guilty side, like she was the one that needed to be forgiven.

"You mustn't mention this to a living soul, Momo. Give me that."

She held out her hand and took the key.

"Madame Rosa, what is this place? Why do you come down here in the middle of the night? What is it?"

She straightened her glasses a little and smiled.

"It's my country home, Momo. Come along."

She blew out the candle and took me by the hand, and we went back upstairs. Then she sat down in the armchair with her hand on her heart, because she couldn't climb the six flights any more without being knocked out.

"Swear you'll never mention it to a living soul, Momo."

"I swear, Madame Rosa."

"*Khaïrem*?"

That means I swear in their language.

"*Khaïrem*."

Then, looking over my head as if she could see far into the distance, she murmured:

"It's my Jewish hideaway, Momo."

"Oh, I see. That's fine."

"Do you understand?"

"No, but that's all right. I'm used to it."

"It's where I hide when I'm afraid."

"Afraid of what, Madame Rosa?"

"You don't need reasons to be afraid, Momo."

I've never forgotten those words, because they were the truest words I've ever heard.

I OFTEN WENT AND SAT IN DR. KATZ'S waiting room, because Madame Rosa kept saying he was a man who did people good, but I never felt any improvement. Maybe I didn't stay long enough. I know there are people who do good in the world, but they don't do it all the time and you've got to come at the right moment, because miracles don't happen. At first Dr. Katz came out and asked me if I was sick, but then he got used to seeing me there and left me alone. Come to think of it, dentists have waiting rooms too, but they only do teeth. Madame Rosa told me Dr. Katz was a general practitioner, and it's true that all kinds of people went to him, Jews naturally same as everywhere else, North Africans, not to say Arabs, black people and all kinds of diseases. He must have had lots of venereal diseases because of the foreign workers who catch them before coming to France so as to cash in on Social Security. Venereal diseases aren't contagious in public and Dr. Katz accepted them, but you weren't allowed to come around with diphtheria, scarlet fever, measles and other diseases that have to be kept at home. Except that the parents didn't always know what was the matter with their kids and once or twice I picked up a case of flu or whooping cough in that waiting room that wasn't meant for me. I came back all the same. I liked sitting in a waiting room waiting for something, and when the door opened and Dr. Katz stepped in, all clad in white, and came over and patted my head I felt better. That's what doctors are for.

Madame Rosa used to worry a lot about my health. She said I was having precocious trouble, meaning what she called the enemy of the human race, which was starting to get big several times a day. Her biggest worry next to precociousness was aunts and uncles, when the real parents get killed in an automobile accident and the next of kin didn't really want to take care of the kids but didn't want to give them to the Public Welfare either, which would have made people think they were heartless in the neighborhood. In cases like that they came to us, especially if the kid was dramatized. Madame Rosa said a child was dramatized when he'd had a drama, as the term indicates. W1hen that happened, he refused to have anything to do with life, a condition known as artistic. It's the worst thing that can happen to a child on top of everything else.

When someone brought her a new kid for a few days or indefinite, Madame Rosa examined him from every angle, but especially to make sure they weren't dramatized. She'd make faces to scare him or put on a glove with a clown on every finger, which always made the kids laugh if they were all right, but if they were dramatized it was like they were dead to the world, and that's why they call that kind of children artistic. Madame

Rosa couldn't take them, they keep you busy day and night, and she didn't have the personnel. One time a Moroccan woman that worked in a whorehouse in the Goutte d'Or section left her a dramatized kid and died without leaving an address. Madame Rosa had to give him to a handicapped organization with forged papers to prove he existed, and she was sick about it, because there's nothing gloomier than an organization.

Even with kids in good health there were risks. You can't force unknown parents to take children back, especially when there's no legal proof against them. There's nothing worse than an unnatural mother. Madame Rosa said the law of the jungle was better than our laws and it was even dangerous to adopt a kid. If the real mother wants to come and torture him later on because he's happy, she's got the law on her side. That's why forged papers are the best way and if some floozy finds out two years later that her kid is happy with his other family, so she wants to get him back and show him what's what, she'll never find him if they've fitted him out with authentic false papers, and that gives him a chance to split.

Madame Rosa used to say animals were a lot better off than we are, because they have the law of nature, especially lionesses. She thought the world of lionesses. Sometimes when I was lying in bed before falling asleep I made the doorbell ring, and when I opened who should it be but a lioness wanting to come in and defend her little ones! Madame Rosa said lionesses were famous for that and they'd sooner be torn to pieces than give an inch of ground. That's the law of the jungle and if a lioness didn't defend her cubs people would lose confidence in her.

I got my lioness to come around almost every night. She'd walk in, she'd jump on the bed and she'd lick our faces, because the others needed it too and I was the oldest, it was my duty to provide for them. But lions have a bad reputation, seeing they've got to eat like everybody else, and when I told the other kids my lioness was coming they began to yell; even Banania started in, and God knows he was hard to faze because of his proverbial good humor. I liked Banania a lot; he was taken by a French family that had room, and I'll go see him one of these days.

In the end Madame Rosa heard that I had a lioness in while she was sleeping. She knew it wasn't true and I was only dreaming about the laws of nature, but she had a very nervous system and the thought of having wild animals in the apartment gave her the heebie-jeebies. She woke up screaming because what was a dream to me was a nightmare to her, and she always said that nightmares are what dreams turn into with age. We dreamed up two entirely different lionesses, but that's the way of the world.

I HAVE NO IDEA WHAT MADAME ROSA dreamed about in general. I don't see what good it does to dream backwards and at her age she couldn't dream forward any more. Maybe she dreamed about her youth, when she was beautiful and had no health to worry about. I don't know what her parents did, but they did it in Poland, and that's where she started hustling, which she continued in Paris, on the rue de Fourcy, the rue Blondel, the rue du Cygne, hither and yon, and then she'd done Morocco and Algeria. She spoke Arabic very well, without prejudice. She'd even done the Foreign Legion at Sidi-bel-Abbès, but her luck changed when she came back to France, because she wanted to taste the sweets of love and the guy took all her savings and denounced her to the French police as a Jewess. At that point in her story she'd always stop and say: "But that's water under the bridge." And she'd smile; she always enjoyed that moment.

When she got back from Germany, she hustled for another few years, but after fifty she began to put on weight and wasn't so appetizing any more. She knew that whores have a hard time keeping their children because the law forbids it for reasons of morality, and that's what gave her the idea of opening a rest home for illegal kids. Luckily for her, one of the first kids she brought up was that police inspector who had a whore for a mother and protected her, but now she was sixty-five, which was to be expected. The thing she was most afraid of was cancer, because cancer has no mercy. I could see she was deteriorating and sometimes we'd look at each other in silence and share our fears, because that's all we had in the world. Which explains why all she needed in her condition was a lioness at large in the apartment. Never mind, I hit on a solution. I'd lie there in the dark with my eyes open, and after a while the lioness would come and lie down beside me and lick my face without a word to anybody. When Madame Rosa woke up in terror, came into our room and made the light reign, she'd see we were sleeping peacefully. But then she'd look under the beds, which was comical when you stop to think that lions were the one thing in the world that couldn't happen to her, seeing that lions are practically nonexistent in Paris, because wild animals live exclusively in nature.

That's when I first realized that she was slightly deranged. She'd had a lot of hard knocks and now she had to pay, because we pay for everything in this life. She even dragged me to Dr. Katz and told him I let wild animals loose in the apartment and that was a sure sign. I knew she and Dr. Katz had something between them they couldn't talk about in front of me, but I had no idea what it was and what Madame Rosa was afraid of.

"Doctor, he's going to do something violent, I just know it."

"Don't talk nonsense, Madame Rosa. You have nothing to fear. Our little Momo is a sensitive, affectionate child. That's not a disease, and take it from an old practitioner, diseases aren't the hardest things to cure."

"Then why has he got lions on the brain?"

"In the first place it's not a lion, it's a lioness."

Dr. Katz smiled and gave me a mint candy.

"It's a lioness. And what do lionesses do? They defend their little ones . . ."

Madame Rosa sighed.

"You know perfectly well what I'm afraid of, Doctor."

Dr. Katz went red in the face with fury.

"Be still, Madame Rosa. You're an utter barbarian. You don't know anything about these things and you imagine God knows what. Such superstitions belong to another age. I've told you that a thousand times. Not another word!"

He was going to say some more but then he looked at me and stood up and sent me out of the room. I had to listen at the keyhole.

"Doctor, I'm afraid he's hereditary."

"That'll do, Madame Rosa, that'll do. In the first place you don't even know who his father was, what with that poor woman's line of work. And anyway, as I've told you, that doesn't mean a thing. There are many other factors to be considered. But one thing is certain: he's a very sensitive child and needs plenty of affection."

"I can't very well lick his face every night, Doctor. Where does he get such ideas? And why wouldn't they keep him at school?"

"Because you gave him a birth certificate out of

all proportion to his real age. You love him, don't you?''

"I'm only afraid they'll take him away from me. Of course they can't prove anything. I take down the information they give me on a scrap of paper or I keep it in my head, because the girls are always afraid of somebody finding out. Prostitutes with corrupted morals forfeit their paternity rights, so they're not allowed to bring up their children. They can be gouged and blackmailed with a kid for years, because they'll agree to anything sooner than lose him. Some procurers are just plain pimps, that's the way it is nowadays, people just aren't serious about their work.''

"You're a fine woman, Madame Rosa. I'll prescribe some tranquilizers.''

I hadn't learned a thing. I was even surer than before that this Jewess was keeping something from me, but I wasn't too keen on finding out. The more you know the worse off you are. My pal Le Mahoute, his mother was a whore too, used to say that mystery was normal with kids like us because of the law of large numbers. He said when a whore who knows her business has an accident and decides to keep it, she always has a social worker hanging over her head, and when that happens you're through. It's always the mother who suffers, because the father's protected by the law of large numbers.

Madame Rosa kept a piece of paper that identified me as Mohammed at the bottom of a suitcase with five pounds of potatoes, a pound of carrots, a quarter of a pound of butter, a smoked herring and three hundred francs, and said to bring me up in the Moslem religion. There was a date, but that was only when she took delivery, and didn't say when I was born.

I was expected to look after the other children, especially to wipe their asses, because it was hard for Madame Rosa to bend down on account of her bulk. She had no waist and her ass went straight up to her shoulders nonstop. Every step she took was like moving a piano.

Every Saturday afternoon she'd put on her blue dress with a fox fur and earrings, paint her face even more than usual and go to a French café, the Coupole at Montparnasse, where she'd eat a piece of cake.

I never wiped the kids' asses when they were past four, because I had my dignity and some of them used to shit on purpose. But I knew those creeps and I taught them a little game, wiping each other's asses, I got them to think it was more fun than each man for himself. It worked fine and Madame Rosa congratulated me; she said I was learning to hold up my end. I didn't play with the other kids, they were too little for me except to compare our peckers, which infuriated Madame Rosa because she'd seen and suffered plenty over the years and peckers gave her a pain. She kept right on being afraid of lions at night, and considering all the other good reasons for being afraid, it's pretty weird to take it out on lions.

Madame Rosa was having trouble with her heart and I did the shopping on account of the stairs. Stairs were the worst thing for her. She wheezed more and more when she breathed, I had asthma myself from sympathy, and Dr. Katz said nothing was more contagious than psychology. It's one of those things that aren't known yet. Every morning I was glad to see Madame Rosa wake up because I had night fears and I was scared pink of being left without her.

My best friend at that time was an umbrella by the name of Arthur. I dressed him from top to toe. I'd made him a head out of a green rag that I rolled around the handle, and a sweet face and round eyes with Madame Rosa's rouge. I needed him less to love than to play the clown with, because I had no pocket money and sometimes I'd go to French neighborhoods where they did. I had a big long overcoat that reached down to my heels and a derby hat, and I'd smear my face with paint. Then I'd go out with my friend Arthur, and we were really comical. I'd pick a good place on the sidewalk and do my monkeyshines, and sometimes I'd take in as much as twenty francs in a day, but I had to watch my step because the police are always on the lookout for minors at large. Arthur was dressed like a one-legged man, with one blue and white basketball shoe, a pair of trousers, a checked jacket on a hanger that I'd tied on with string and a round hat that I'd sewn on his head. I'd asked Monsieur N'Da Amédée to lend me clothes for my umbrella and do you know what he did? He took me to the Golden Gaiters on the Boulevard de Belleville, which is a temple of fashion, and let me pick whatever I wanted. I don't know if they're all like him in Africa, but if they are I can guarantee that they want for nothing.

Then I'd do my act. I'd prance and strut and dance with Arthur and pick up the change. Some of the people were good and mad, they said it was disgraceful to treat a child like that. I couldn't make out who was treating me like what, but those people looked really down in the mouth. Which was funny, because my idea was to make them laugh.

Arthur got broken now and then. I put nails in the coat hanger, which gave him shoulders, and one of his trouser legs was always empty, which is normal for an umbrella. Monsieur Hamil didn't like it at all. He said Arthur looked like a fetish and fetishes were against our religion. I'm not religious myself, but it's true that if you've got something weird that doesn't look like anything else you can't help hoping it will do something for you. I'd sleep with Arthur clutched in my arms and in the morning I'd look to see if Madame Rosa was still breathing.

I've never been in a church because it's against the true religion and the last thing in the world I wanted was that kind of trouble. But I knew for a fact that the Christians paid through the nose for their plaster Christs, when in our religion it's forbidden to represent the human face on pain of offending God, which makes sense because it's really nothing to brag about. So I was kind of scared and wiped Arthur's face off, all I left was a green ball, green as with envy, which squared me with my religion. Once when the cops were after me because I'd drawn an unlawful assembly with

my act, I dropped Arthur and he scattered in all
directions, hat, hanger, jacket, shoe and all. I
managed to pick him up, but he was as naked as
the Lord made him. Well, the funny part of it is
that Madame Rosa hadn't said a word when I
slept with Arthur in his clothes, but once he was
defrocked she yelled bloody murder when I started
taking him under the covers with me, and said
who ever heard of going to bed with an umbrella.
That's a hard one to understand.

I'd saved up some money and I got Arthur a
new outfit at the Flea Market, where they have
some pretty nice things.

But our luck began to fail us.

My money orders had always been irregular;
they skipped a month now and then, but they
always came in the end. All of a sudden they
stopped. Two months, three months, nothing.
Four months.

"Don't be afraid," I said to Madame Rosa.
"You can count on me. I'm not going to drop you
just because the money stops coming." I was so
sincere that my voice trembled. After that I took
Arthur and sat on the sidewalk because I didn't
want to cry at home.

Take it from me, our situation was rotten. The
age limit was creeping up on Madame Rosa and
she knew it. The six flights of stairs were her
public enemy number one. She was sure they'd kill
her one of these days. It wouldn't have taken
much killing, you had only to look at her. Her
breasts, belly and ass were like a barrel, all one
piece without distinction. We had fewer and fewer
boarders because the whores were put off by

Madame Rosa's health. They saw she was in no condition to take care of anybody, so they preferred to pay more and go to Madame Sophie or Mother Fatma on the rue d'Alger. They were taking in plenty of money, so why not? Madame Rosa's personal coterie of whores were gone with the generation gap. Everybody knew she lived from mouth to mouth, so the girls had stopped recommending her to each other, and she was losing her reputation. As long as her legs would carry her, she'd visit them on their sidewalks or in the cafés where they hung out and advertise her establishment, the first-class accommodations, the culinary cooking, and so on. But she couldn't do that any more. Her girl friends were all gone and with them her references. And besides they'd legalized the pill for the protection of childhood, so you really had to want kids and have them on purpose. If you had a kid now, there was no excuse, you knew what you were doing to him.

I was at least ten or pretty near, and it was up to me to help Madame Rosa. I had to think of my own future, because if I was left alone it was the Public Welfare and no come-back. I'd lie awake at night thinking about it and looking at Madame Rosa to see if she was still alive.

I tried hustling. I'd give my hair a good combing and put some of Madame Rosa's perfume behind my ears like she did. Then I'd take Arthur and mosey down to the rue Pigalle or maybe the rue Blanche, which is pretty good too. You'll find women working those sidewalks at any time of day, and one or two of them would come over to me.

"My goodness," they'd say. "What a cute little man! Does your mother work here?"

"No, I haven't got anybody yet."

They'd treat me to a mint drink at the café on the rue Macé. But I had to keep my eyes open because the police are always on the lookout for procurers and the girls had to be careful too, because they're not allowed to accost people. It was always the same questions.

"How old are you, sweetie?"

"Have you got a mother?"

I said no and I felt bad for Madame Rosa, but what could I do? There was one who used to pet me especially and now and then she'd slip a bill into my pocket as she passed. She wore a mini-skirt and boots up to the waist and she was younger than Madame Rosa. She had real friendly eyes. One time she took a good look around and took me by the hand. We went to a café that isn't there any more because somebody threw a bomb into it, the Panier.

"You shouldn't hang around here. It's no place for a kid."

She patted my hair to put it in order, but I knew it was patting for patting's sake.

"What's your name?"

"Momo."

"Where are your parents, Momo?"

"I haven't got anybody. What do you think? I'm free."

"But you must have somebody to look after you."

I sipped my orangeade, waiting to see what would come of it.

"I'd be glad to take care of you, Momo. I'll set you up in a nice little apartment. You'll live like a prince. You'll want for nothing."

"I'll see."

I finished my orangeade and slid off my chair.

"Well, anyway, sweetie, take this for candy."

She slipped a bill into my pocket. A hundred francs.

I went back two or three times, she always greeted me with a big smile, but sad and from a distance, because I wasn't hers.

My hard luck, the cashier at the Panier was an old friend of Madame Rosa's, they'd walked the streets together. She told her all about it, and boy what a scene she treated me to. Flagrant jealousy, that's what it was. I'd never seen her in such a state. "Is this what I raised you for?" she kept saying through her tears. I had to swear I'd never go back and never turn procurer as long as I lived. She said they were common pimps every last one of them and she'd sooner be dead. But what other career was open to me at the age of ten?

What's always struck me as funny is that tears are built in. I mean humans were designed to cry. What a goofy idea! No self-respecting designer would have done that.

There were still no money orders and Madame Rosa started tapping the savings bank. She'd put a little money aside for her old age, but she knew she couldn't last long. She didn't have cancer yet but everything else was deteriorating fast. She even talked to me about my mother and father for the first time, because it seems there were two of them. They'd come and deposited me one evening and it seems my mother had started bawling and left on the run. Madame Rosa put me down as Mohammed, Moslem, and promised I'd live like a king. And then what? Well, then she'd sigh, and that was all she knew, except she never looked me in the eye when she said that. I didn't know what she was keeping from me but it scared me at night. I never got anything more out of her, not even when the money orders stopped coming and she had no more reason to be kind to me. All I knew was that I had a mother and a father, because in that respect nature doesn't do things by halves. But they had never come back and Madame Rosa just clammed up and looked guilty. I can tell you right now that I never found my mother, because I wouldn't want to raise any false hopes. Once when I pestered her, Madame Rosa made up such a nice lie it was really a pleasure.

"If you ask me, your mother had old-fashioned ideas—she came of a good family, you see. She didn't want you to know her profession. So broken-hearted she crept away, sobbing and never to return, because knowing your mother was a whore would have given you a dramatic shock, that's the law of psychology."

And then she herself would burst into tears. Nobody loved a touching story more than Madame Rosa. I think Dr. Katz was right. When I talked to him about it, he said whores were only a state of mind. So did Monsieur Hamil, who'd read Victor Hugo and seen more of life than any other man of his age. He smiled and said that nothing is black or white, that whiteness is often a blackness that hides itself and blackness is sometimes a whiteness that's been had. And with a look at Monsieur Driss, who'd just brought him his mint tea, he'd add: "Trust my long experience." Monsieur Hamil is a great man but the circumstances wouldn't let him become one.

No MONEY ORDERS HAD COME FOR months and Madame Rosa had never seen the color of Banania's money except the day he landed and then she'd insisted on two months' board in advance. Banania was going on four free of charge and behaving as free and easy as if he'd paid up. But that kid had always been lucky and in the end Madame Rosa found him a family. Moïse was still under observation, he took his meals with the Jewish family that had been observing him for six months to make sure he was high-grade and free from epilepsy and fits of violence. Fits of violence are what families are most afraid of in a child, and they're the first thing to avoid if you want to get yourself adopted. To feed the day boarders and Madame Rosa we needed twelve hundred francs a month, not to mention medical expenses and the credit nobody would give us. You couldn't even have fed Madame Rosa all by herself on less than fifteen francs a day without committing atrocities, even on a reducing diet. I remember, I told her frankly one day that she'd have to reduce to eat less, but it's very hard for an old woman that's all alone in the world. She needs to have more of herself than other people. When there's nobody to love you, it turns to fat. I started going back to Pigalle; that lady, Maryse, was still there, she was in love with me because I was still a child. But I was scared because they put procurers in jail and we had to meet on the q.t. I'd wait for her in a doorway, she'd come over and bend down and hug me and kiss me. "Sweet little darling," she'd say. "How I wish I had a son like you," and then she'd slip me the price of a trick.

And then I worked out a little shoplifting scheme in the neighborhood. I'd take Banania and leave him alone with his smile in the middle of a self-service store to disarm the public and draw a crowd, because of the tender feelings he inspired. Blacks are affectionately tolerated when they're four or five years old. Sometimes I'd pinch him to make him yell, the people would crowd around him with curiosity and compassion and meanwhile I'd swipe useful things to eat. I had an overcoat that reached down to my heels with big quick-disappearing pockets Madame Rosa had made. Hunger is a good teacher. To get out of the store, I'd pick Banania up in my arms and station myself behind some lady in the pay line; the cashier would think I was with the lady and Banania would roll his eyes and look cute. Children are very popular before they get to the dangerous age. People would smile and say nice things even to me, it always comforts them to see a kid who's too young to be a genuine thug. I have brown hair and blue eyes and my nose isn't Jewish like an Arab; I could have been anything at all without changing my face.

Madame Rosa began to eat less, it was good for her and for us too. Besides, we had more and more kids, it was the summer season and people were going further and further on their vacation. I'd never been happier to wipe asses, because they made the kettle boil, and I didn't even mind having my fingers full of shit.

Unfortunately, Madame Rosa was disintegrating; the laws of nature were attacking her on every side, in the legs, the eyes, the vital organs such as the heart, liver and arteries, and everything else that happens to people when they're badly used up. Some days, seeing there was no elevator, she'd collapse on the stairs, and we'd all have to go down and push her, even Banania, who was beginning to wake up to life and realize that even he had an interest in protecting his daily bread.

The most important parts of a person are the heart and head, and they're the most costly. If the heart stops, you can't go on as usual, and if the head detaches itself from everything and refuses to function properly, the person loses his facilities and can't hope to get anything out of life. I believe that if you want to live, you should start very young, because later on you're sure to depreciate and no one will make you any presents.

Sometimes I'd bring Madame Rosa things I'd pick up without the slightest utility, that were no good for anything but gave pleasure because nobody wanted them and they'd been thrown away. Some people, for instance bring flowers home because it's somebody's birthday or for no reason at all, just to cheer up the apartment; then when they dry out and lose their first flush, they throw them in the garbage and if you get up very early you can rescue them. These so-called castoffs were my specialty. Sometimes there's a little color left and they have a little longer to live. I'd make up bouquets regardless of their age and give them to Madame Rosa, who'd put them in vases without water, because it's no use by that time. Or I'd swipe whole armfuls of mimosa off the market carts and take them home to bring in the smell of happiness. As I carried them through the streets, I'd dream of the battles of flowers in Nice and the mimosa forests which surround that gleaming white city that Monsieur Hamil had known in his youth and still spoke of now and then, though he wasn't the same any more.

We spoke mostly Yiddish and Arabic between ourselves, or French when there were strangers present or we didn't want to be understood, but lately Madame Rosa had started mixing all the languages of her life and talking to me in Polish, her earliest language, that was coming back to her now, because what sticks to old people the longest is their youth. Well, anyway, she was still managing to hold on, except for the stairs, but it wasn't easy and she needed shots in the ass. It was hard to find a nurse young enough to climb the six flights or reasonably low-priced. I made an arrangement with Le Mahoute, who needled legally because he had diabetes and the state of his health permitted it. He was a good kid, who was self-made but mostly black and Algerian. He sold transistors and other stuff he'd stolen, and the rest of the time he'd try to get cured of his hang-up at the Marmottan Hospital, where he had his ins and outs. He turned up all right for Madame Rosa's shot, but we almost came to grief, because he got the ampules mixed and shot Madame Rosa's ass full of the heroin fix he'd saved for the day when his cure would be over.

I knew right away there was something fishy, because I'd never seen Madame Rosa so blissful. The first thing that hit her was amazement, and then the bliss took hold. Frankly, she had me worried; she was so far gone in heaven I thought she'd never come back. I say, to hell with junk. The kids who take it all get addicted to happiness, and that's the end, because happiness is famous for the misery of going without it. Anybody who takes drugs must really want to be happy, and who would do that but a king or a dope? I've never touched the hard stuff, only smoked grass a few times with the boys to be polite, and that's all, though ten is the age when the big guys come around teaching you all sorts of things. But happiness doesn't mean much to me, I still think life is better. Happiness is a mean son of a bitch and needs to be put in his place. Him and me aren't on the same team, and I'm cutting him dead. I've never gone in for politics, because somebody always stands to gain by it, but happiness is an even crummier racket, and there ought to be laws to put it out of business. I'm only telling you what I think, and maybe I'm wrong, but you won't catch me shooting myself full of happiness, or shit as I prefer to call it. I won't say another word about it, because I don't want to throw one of my violent fits, but Monsieur Hamil says I have a gift for the ineffable, which is where happiness is and that's the place to look for it.

The best way to get shit, and that's what Le

Mahoute did, was to say you'd never taken any and then the pushers give you a fix free of charge because misery loves company. The number of pushers who've wanted to break me in is unbelievable, but I'm not here to solve other people's problems, I had my hands full with Madame Rosa. I have no intention of plunging into happiness until I've tried everything else.

So Le Mahoute—the name doesn't mean a thing, that's why it stuck to him—shot Madame Rosa full of heroin. First Madame Rosa was stricken with amazement, then she went into a state of satisfaction that was horrible to look at. Think it over, sixty-five and Jewish—that was all she needed. I ran for Dr. Katz, because with heroin there's a danger of what they call overdoze, and you end up in an artificial paradise. Dr. Katz didn't come, because he was too old and forbidden to climb the six flights except in case of death. But he phoned a young doctor he knew, who turned up an hour later. Madame Rosa was drooling in her armchair. The doctor looked at me as if he'd never seen a ten-year-old kid.

"What is this place? Some sort of nursery?"

I felt sorry for him standing there so indignant. He just couldn't believe it. Le Mahoute was on the floor, bawling because he'd shot happiness into Madame Rosa's ass.

"How could such a thing happen? Who supplied this old lady with heroin?"

I looked at him with my hands in my pockets. I smiled at him but I didn't say anything. What was the use? He was so young, maybe thirty, and still had so much to learn.

A FEW DAYS LATER SOMETHING NICE happened to me. I had some business in one of the department stores near the Opera, where they had a circus in the window, so parents could bring their kids with no obligation on their part. I'd already seen it ten times but that day I got there too early, they hadn't raised the curtain yet, so I chewed the fat for a while with an African street sweeper. I didn't know him but he was black and he came from Aubervilliers, because there are black people there too. We smoked a cigarette and I watched him sweeping the sidewalk for a while, because that was the best thing to do. Then I went back to the store and feasted my eyes. The window was framed in over-life-sized stars that lit up and went out as fast as you can blink. The circus was in the middle with clowns and cosmonauts that went to the moon and back, waving at the passers-by, and acrobats flying through the air with professional ease, white dancing girls riding in tutus on horseback, and strong men with bulging muscles lifting unbelievable weights without batting an eyelash, because they weren't human and it was done by machinery. There was even a camel that danced and a magician with a hat that had rabbits coming out of it in Indian file; they marched once around the ring and then got back into the hat and started all over again, because it was a continuous performance that couldn't stop even if it wanted to. The clowns were all colors and dressed the way it's compulsory for clowns, blue and white and rainbow colors, with a red light bulb for a nose that lighted up. In back there was a big audience, not real people, just mechanical, who applauded the whole time, because that's what they were made for. There was a space ship and when the cosmonaut reached the moon, he stood up and waved, and the French flag went up. When you thought you'd seen it all, a bunch of comical elephants came out of their garage, holding each other by the tail, and walked around the ring. The last in line was still a baby, all pink as if he'd just been born. But for my money the clowns were the thing. They weren't like anything else in the world. Their faces were fantastic, with eyes like question marks, and they were so idiotic they were always in a good humor. I looked at them and I thought how funny Madame Rosa would have been if she'd been a clown, but she wasn't, and that was the rotten part of it. They had pants that fell down and came up again because they were so uproarious and musical instruments that gave off sparks and streams of water instead of what those instruments gave off in everyday life. There were four clowns, and the head clown was white with a pointed hat and baggy pants and his face even whiter than all the rest of him. The others bowed and scraped and saluted him, and he kicked them in the ass, that's all he did the whole time, he couldn't have stopped

even if he'd wanted to, because he'd been set that
way. There was a yellow clown with green spots
and a face that was always happy even when he
fell on it. He did a tightrope number and bungled
it every time, but he seemed to enjoy it, because he
was philosophical. He had a red wig that stood on
end when he put his first foot on the wire, and he
couldn't go forward or back, and he started trembling to make people laugh with fright, because
there's nothing funnier than a scared clown. His
sidekick was all blue and very nice, he had a mini-
guitar and he sang to the moon, and you could see
he had a very good heart but couldn't help it. The
last one was really two, because he had a double
and everything one did the other had to do, they
tried to resist, but they couldn't, because they
were connected. The best part of it was that the
whole thing was mechanical and good-natured,
you knew in advance that they couldn't suffer or
grow old, and that nothing ever went wrong. It
was entirely different from everything else in the
world. Even the camel was friendly, contrary to
his reputation. His whole face was one big smile
and he waggled his ass like a lady. Everybody was
happy in that circus and there was nothing natural
about it. The clown walked the tightrope in perfect security, in ten days I didn't see him fall once,
and even if he'd fallen I knew he couldn't hurt
himself. It was really different, see. I was so happy
I wanted to die, because you've got to grab happiness when it's there.

So I was happily watching the circus when I felt
a hand on my shoulder. I thought it was a cop and
turned around fast, but it was a chick, not too old,

twenty-five at the most. She was not bad, blond,
with her hair hanging loose, and she smelled sweet
and fresh.

"Why are you crying?"

"I'm not crying."

She touched my cheek.

"Then what's this? Not tears?"

"No. I don't know where it comes from."

"All right. I see I was mistaken. Isn't it a lovely
circus?"

"Best thing of its kind I've ever seen."

"Do you live around here?"

"No, I'm not French. I'm probably Algerian,
we live in Belleville."

"What's your name?"

"Momo."

I couldn't see what she was picking me up for.
A ten-year-old is no good for anything, not even if
he's an Arab. She kept her hand on my cheek and
I moved back a bit. You've got to be careful. You
may not know it, but there are social workers who
look perfectly innocent and before you know it
they give you a summons that ends in an in-
vestigation. There's nothing worse than an in-
vestigation. Madame Rosa couldn't sleep at night
thinking about them. I moved back a little more
but not too much, just enough to beat it if she
tried to grab me. But she was awfully pretty, she
could have made a fortune if she'd wanted to with
a good hard-working pimp to look after her. She
started to laugh.

"There's nothing to be afraid of."

Are you kidding? "There's nothing to be afraid
of." What a dumb thing to say! Monsieur Hamil

always says that fear is our surest friend and God alone knows what would happen to us without it, trust my long experience. Monsieur Hamil was so scared that he even went to Mecca.

"You shouldn't be on the streets all alone at your age."

That handed me a laugh. I really split my sides internally. But I didn't let on, it wasn't my job to teach her the facts of life.

"You're the handsomest little boy I've ever seen."

"You're not bad yourself."

She laughed.

"Thank you."

I don't know what got into me, I conceived a ray of hope. Not that I was thinking of moving in with her. I wasn't going to run out on Madame Rosa as long as she could hold her own. But all the same I had to think of the future, which is sure to smack you in the face sooner or later. Somebody with vacations on the seashore, who wouldn't make me feel bad, sometimes I dreamed about it at night. All right, I was slightly unfaithful to Madame Rosa, but only in my head, when I wanted to die. I looked at her hopefully and my heart pounded. Hope always gets the best of you, even with old people like Madame Rosa or Monsieur Hamil. No sense to it.

But she didn't say any more. It stopped there. People are weird. She talked to me, she paid me a compliment, she gave me a sweet smile, and then she sighed and went away. A bitch.

She was wearing a raincoat and slacks. Even from behind I could see her blond hair. She was slender and I could see by the way she walked that she could have run up and down the six flights several times a day with bundles.

I followed her because I had nothing better to do. Once she stopped and saw me, and we both laughed. Once I hid in a doorway, but she didn't turn around and she didn't come back. I pretty near lost her. She was walking fast and I think she'd forgotten me because she had fish to fry. She went into a building and I saw her stop on the ground floor and ring a bell. What would you expect? The door opened and two kids jumped on her neck. Seven or eight years old. Honest to God!

I sat down in the entrance and stayed there a while.

I didn't want very much to be there or anywhere else. There were two or three things I could have done. There was the drugstore at the Étoile with the comic books; with comic books you can forget your own troubles and everybody else's. Or I could have gone to see the girls who were sweet on me at Pigalle and made a little money. But all of a sudden I was fed up and didn't care where I was. I didn't want to be anywhere at all. I shut my eyes, but it takes more than that; I was still there, it's automatic when you're alive. I couldn't see why that bitch had made up to me. I have to admit I'm kind of a dope that way, always trying to understand things. Monsieur Hamil is right when he says that nobody has understood anything for centuries and one can only stand amazed. I went back to the circus and gained an hour or two, but that's nothing in a day. I went to a tearoom for ladies and ate two pastries, chocolate eclairs, that's what

I like best. Then I asked where I could piss and when I came back up, I beat it straight to the door, bye-bye. After that I swiped a pair of gloves off a counter at the Printemps and threw them in a garbage can. That made me feel better.

ON MY WAY BACK SOMETHING REALLY extraordinary happened on the rue de Ponthieu. I don't really believe in extraordinary things, because I can't see what's so different about them.

I was afraid to go home. Madame Rosa was a dismal sight and I knew she was going to pass away on me from one minute to the next. I was always thinking about it and sometimes I didn't dare to go home. I had a good mind to swipe something big in one of the stores and get pinched just to show how I felt. Or get cornered in a bank vault and defend myself to the last gasp with a tommy gun. But whatever I did I knew no one would pay attention. So I was on the rue de Ponthieu and I killed an hour or two watching some guys playing Baby Foot in a bar. Then I wanted to go somewhere else but I didn't know where, so I just hung around. I knew Madame Rosa would be eating her heart out, she was always afraid of something happening to me. She hardly ever went out, because you couldn't get her back up the stairs any more. At first four or five of us would wait on the sidewalk, and when she got back we'd all get together and push her up. But now it was more and more seldom, she hadn't enough strength left in her legs or heart, or wind enough for a person half her size and weight. She wouldn't hear of going to a hospital, because in the hospital they let you die to the bitter end, instead of giving you a shot. She said they were against mercy killing in France and forced you to live as long as you were capable of suffering. Madame Rosa was scared to death of torture; she always said that when she really had her belly full she'd get abortioned. She warned us that if the hospital got hold of her we'd all be taken legally to the Public Welfare, and she'd burst into tears at the thought of dying in the arms of the law. The law, she said, was made to protect the people with something to protect from other people. Monsieur Hamil says that humankind is no more than a comma in the great Book of Life, and when an old man says something as dumb as that, I don't see what the likes of me can add. Humankind is certainly not a comma, because when Madame Rosa looks at me with those Jewish eyes of hers she's no comma, she's more like the whole big Book of Life, and I don't want to see it. I went to the mosque twice to help Madame Rosa, but it didn't do her a bit of good, because it doesn't work for Jews. That's why I didn't want to go back to Belleville and find myself eye to eye with Madame Rosa. She was always saying, *"Oeil! Oeil!"*, that's the Jewish exclamation when they hurt somewhere, with the Arabs it's entirely different, we say, *"Khaï! Khaï!"*, and the French say, *"Oh! Oh!"* when they're unhappy, because they are sometimes, you're wrong if you think they're not. I was going on ten when Madame Rosa decided that I should get in the habit of having a date of birth, and it was that very day. She said it was important for my normal development but that all the rest, father's name, mother's name, and all that, was pretentious nonsense.

I sat in a doorway and waited for the time to pass, but time is even older than everything else and moves very slowly. When people are in pain, their eyes get big and make more expression than before. Madame Rosa's eyes were getting bigger and more and more like the look in a dog's eyes when somebody beats him and he doesn't know why. I could see her plain as day, even if she was at home and I was on the rue de Ponthieu, near the Champs-Élysées, where the quality stores are. More and more she was losing the hair she had before the war, and when she was feeling well enough to stick up for herself, she kept after me to find her a new wig with real hair that would make her look like a woman. Her old wig was a wreck, and so was she. I can't deny it, she was getting as bald as a man, and the sight gave you sore eyes, because women weren't designed for it. She wanted another red wig, that was the color best suited to her kind of beauty. But where was I going to steal one? In Belleville we didn't have any of those establishments for ugly women known as beauty parlors. On the Champs-Élysées I was afraid to go in. You've got to tell them what you want and give them the measurements and all that.

I was feeling low. I didn't even want a Coke. I tried to tell myself that I hadn't been born that day any more than any other day and that all this business about dates of birth was only a collective convention anyway. I thought of my pals, Le Mahoute or the Shah, who worked in a filling station. When you're a kid, you've got to be more than one to amount to anything.

I lay down on the ground, closed my eyes and did exercises to make me die, but the cement was cold and I was afraid of catching cold. In my situation I know kids who'd shoot themselves full of shit, but I'm not the kind that licks life's ass for the sake of happiness. You won't catch me putting ribbons on life, I say, to hell with it. We have nothing to offer each other. Maybe when I'm a major I'll be a terrorist and hijack planes and take hostages like on TV, and demand things, I haven't decided what, but it won't be peanuts. The big time, see? But right now I don't know what demands to make, because I haven't had the professional training.

I was lying there with my ass on the cement, hijacking planes and taking hostages who trooped out with their hands up, and wondering what to do with the money, because you can't buy everything. I'll buy real estate for Madame Rosa, so she can die in peace in a seaside villa with a new wig. I'll send whores and their kids to palace hotels in Nice, where life can't come near them and maybe when they grow up they'll be chiefs of state on an official visit to Paris or pillars of national democracy. I'll even be able to buy that TV set I just saw in the store window.

I was thinking about all that but I wasn't really in the mood for business. I dreamed up the blue clown and we had a nice chat. Then I brought in the white clown, and he sat down beside me and played a little silence on his mini-violin. I had a good mind to cross over and stay with them for good, but I couldn't leave Madame Rosa all alone in the shit. We'd taken in a new *café au lait* Viet instead of the old one that a French West Indian black woman had had on purpose by a boyfriend whose mother was Jewish and she wanted to bring him up herself, because she'd loved the guy. She paid cash on the line because Monsieur N'Da Amédée let her keep enough money for a decent life. He took 40 per cent of their earnings, because it was a very busy sidewalk that never stopped, and he had to pay off the Yugoslavs, who are a terrible headache with their rackets. The Corsicans also had to have their cut, because a younger generation was springing up and everything was changing.

There was a basket full of unnecessary objects near where I was lying. I could have set fire to it and the whole building would have gone up in smoke, but nobody would have known it was me, and besides it would have been dangerous. I remember that particular moment so well because it was exactly like all other moments. As far as I'm concerned, everyday life goes on day after day, but sometimes I feel even worse. I had no excuse, I didn't hurt anywhere, but I felt as if I had neither arms nor legs when, if the truth be known, I had plenty of both. Even Monsieur Hamil couldn't have told me why.

Without wanting to hurt anyone's feelings, I've got to admit that Monsieur Hamil was getting more and more gaga, which is sometimes the case with old people who are so far gone they really have no more excuse for being around. They know what to expect, and you can see by their eyes that they're looking backward, hiding their heads in the past like ostriches with a policy. He still carried his book of Victor Hugo around with him, but he was hazy in his mind and thought it was the Koran, because he had both. He knew them both by heart in little snatches and they flowed out of him like water, but mixed. When I went to the mosque with him, where we made an excellent impression because I led him like a blind man and our people have a weakness for the blind, he was always getting mixed up and reciting "Waterloo, Waterloo, dismal plain" instead of praying, which startled the Arabs there assembled, because it was out of place. His religious fervor actually brought the tears to his eyes. He was a fine figure in his gray djellaba with the white *galmona* on his head, and he'd pray for a good reception up there. But he never died, a distinction that few can claim at his age, and I wouldn't be surprised if he got to be the all-category world champion. In the human race it's dogs that die youngest. By the time they're twelve, you can't expect much and my advice is to turn them in. The next time I get a dog I'll take him out of his cradle, that will give me plenty of time to lose him. Clowns are the only people who have no problem of life and death, seeing they're not born in the family way. They were invented free from the laws of nature, and they never die, because that wouldn't be funny. I can see them right before my eyes when I want to. I can see anybody I want right before my eyes, King Kong or Frankenstein, or a flock of wounded pink birds, all except my mother, my imagination isn't good enough for that.

I got up, I was sick of that doorway, and looked out into the street to see what I could see. There was a police bus on the right, and a lot of cops all ready for action. I'd like to be a cop myself when I'm a major, because then I won't be afraid of nothing or nobody and I'll know what to do, because when you're a cop you've got authority on top of you. Madame Rosa used to say that a lot of whores' kids from the Public Welfare get to be cops and riot police and Republican Guards, and after that they're untouchable.

I looked around with my hands in my pockets and went over to the police bus. I was kind of scared. They weren't all in the bus, some had dispersed themselves on the street. I started whistling "On the Highroads of Lorraine," because I don't look like a French kid, and right away one of them started smiling at me.

Cops have the biggest clout of anybody. If a kid has a cop for a father, it's like having twice as many fathers as other kids. They accept Arabs and even black men, if there's something French about them. They're all whores' kids raised by the Public Welfare, and no one can teach them anything. There's no better security force, that's my frank opinion. Even Army soldiers aren't knee-high to them, except maybe a general. Madame Rosa is scared to death of cops, but that's because of the home where she was exterminated in Germany, which cuts no dice because she was on the wrong side. Or I'll go to Algeria and join the police, because that's where they're needed most. There aren't nearly as many Algerians in France as in Algeria, so naturally there's less for them to do over here. I took another step or two toward the bus. They were all waiting for riots or armed robbery, and my heart was pounding. I always feel illegal, I know I have no right to be around. But they didn't lift a finger, maybe they were tired. One was asleep at the window, another was calmly eating a banana with a transistor, all very relaxed. Outside the bus there was a cop with a walkie-talkie who didn't seem the least bit worried. I was scared, but it was good to be afraid and know why, because usually I'm scared silly for no reason at all, it comes as natural as breathing. The cop with the walkie-talkie saw me but he took no action and I walked past him whistling like I owned the place.

Some cops are married and have kids, I know it for a fact. One time I tried to discuss the question with Le Mahoute; what was it like to have a cop for a father? But he wouldn't have anything to do with it, said there was no sense in dreaming, and split. You can't discuss anything with a hophead. No curiosity.

I wandered around some more to keep from going home, counting the steps from one corner to another. Some of those blocks were enormous, my numbers didn't go that far. There was still some sun. Some day I'm going to the country to see what it's like. The sea might interest me too, Monsieur Hamil thinks very highly of it. I don't know what would have become of me without Monsieur Hamil, who taught me everything I know. He came to France with an uncle when he was a kid, his uncle died when he was very young, but he managed to qualify all the same. Now he's getting more and more gaga, but that's because people aren't designed to live so long. The sun looked like a yellow clown sitting on a roof. I'll go to Mecca some day, Monsieur Hamil says there's more sun there than anywhere else, that's on account of geography. But I suspect that in other respects even Mecca isn't so very elsewhere. I wish I could go a long long way, to a place that's full of something different. I don't even try to imagine what it's like because that would spoil it. I guess I'd hold on to clowns, dogs and the sun, because it would be hard to do better in their line. But all the rest would be absolutely unknown and specially designed for that purpose. But even then I bet it would manage to be the same. Sometimes you've got to laugh at the way things tend to stay put.

IT WAS FIVE O'CLOCK AND I WAS
starting for home when I saw a blonde stopping
her mini on the sidewalk, under the no-parking
sign. I recognized her right away, because when I
get a grudge I keep it warm. It was the floozy I'd
followed for nothing after she'd made up to me
and dropped me. I was really surprised to see her.
There's lots of streets in Paris and you've got to be
lucky to meet somebody by accident. She hadn't
seen me because I was on the other side of the
street, so I crossed over quick. But she was in a
hurry or maybe she'd forgotten me, because at
least two hours had passed. She went into No. 39,
which had a court inside with another building on
it. I didn't even have time to get her attention. She
was wearing a camel's hair coat and pants, with
lots of hair on her head, all blond. She'd left a
trail of perfume at least fifteen feet long. She
hadn't locked her car and at first I wanted to
swipe something out of it to make her sit up and
take notice, but I had such a load of blues on
account of my birth date and all, that I don't see
where I found room for it. It was too much for
one kid all by himself. Hell, I thought, what's the
use of taking anything, she won't even know it's
me. I wanted her to see me, but you mustn't think

I was looking for a family, Madame Rosa would last a while, if she really tried. Moïse had found a home and Banania was in the bargaining stage with a family, so I had nothing to worry about. I had no known sicknesses and I wasn't misadjusted, that's the first thing people worry about when they're looking you over. I can see their point, because families take you on trust and the next thing they know they're stuck with a child of alcoholic parentage and arrested development, when there are plenty of flawless specimens that haven't found a buyer. Same here, if I'd had my choice, I'd have picked the best, and not a broken-down old Jewess, who made me want to die every time I saw the state she was in. If Madame Rosa had been a dog, she'd already have been put out of her misery, but people are much nicer to dogs than to human beings, who aren't allowed to die without suffering. I'm telling you this because I wouldn't want you to think my purpose in following Mademoiselle Nadine, as she was called, was to let Madame Rosa die in peace.

THE ENTRANCE OF THE BUILDING LED
to a second smaller building, and as soon as I went
in I heard shots, screeching brakes, a woman
screaming, and a man begging somebody: "Don't
kill me! Don't kill me!" It was so near me I
jumped sky-high. A second later I heard a burst
from a tommy gun, and the man yelled: "No!
No!" the way people do when they die without
wanting to. Then there was a long silence that was
even more awful and what happened next you
won't believe. The whole thing started all over
again with the same bozo who didn't want to be
killed because he had his reasons and the tommy
gun that wouldn't listen. Like it or not, he had to
die three times. I guessed he was a really far-out
bastard and they had to kill him three times as an
example to posterity. Then there was another
silence, during which he stayed dead. After that
they mowed him down a fourth and a fifth time.
In the end you couldn't help feeling sorry for him,
because what the hell. Then they stopped killing
him, and a woman's voice said: "My darling, my
poor darling," with so much quivering and sincere
sentiment that I was all agog, whatever that
means. There was nobody in the entrance but me
and a door with a red light that was on. I'd hardly

gotten my breath back when they started all over again with "My darling, my darling," but each time in a different tone of voice, and they kept doing it over and over again. The bozo had to die five or six times in the arms of his floozy. I guess it gave him a kick to feel that his expiration made somebody unhappy. I thought of Madame Rosa, who didn't have anybody to say "my darling, my poor darling" to because she had practically no hair left and weighed about two hundred and twenty pounds, all of them very unattractive. Then the floozy stopped talking but just in time to let out such a cry of despair that I rushed in as one man. Damned if it wasn't some kind of movie, except that everybody was walking backwards. The floozy on the screen fell on the corpse's body and agonized over him, then a second later she got up, but in reverse and did everything backwards, like she'd been alive on the way in and a doll on the way out. Then the screen went black and they switched on the light.

THE CHICK WHO'D RUN OUT ON ME was standing at the front of the room with a mike when the lights went on, and she saw me. There were three or four guys in the corners but they weren't armed. I must have looked like a dope with my mouth open, because everybody was staring at me. The blonde recognized me and gave me a big smile, which helped my morale a little, seeing I'd made an impression on her.

"Hey, it's my friend!"

We weren't friends at all, but I wasn't going to argue. She came up to me and looked at Arthur, but I knew it was me she was interested in. Sometimes women make me laugh.

"Who's this?"

"An old umbrella I dressed up."

"He's cute. That suit makes him look like a fetish. Is he your pal?"

"Do you think I'm retarded or what? He's not a pal, he's an umbrella."

She took Arthur and pretended to look at him. So did the others. The first thing nobody wants when they adopt a kid is for him to be retarded. That means a kid who has decided to stop along the way, because he doesn't like the looks of the prospects. When that happens, you get handicapped parents and they don't know what to do with him. For instance, a kid is fifteen but acts like ten. The trouble is, you can't win. When a kid is ten like me and acts like fifteen, they say he's disturbed and throw him out of school.

"He's sweet with his little green face. Why did you make his face green?"

She smelled so good I thought of Madame Rosa because of the big difference.

"It's not a face, it's a rag. We're not allowed to have faces."

"Not allowed? What do you mean?"

She had smiling eyes, pretty nice, and she was squatting down in front of Arthur, but she meant me.

"I'm an Arab. Faces aren't allowed in our religion."

"Representations of faces, you mean?"

"It's offensive to God."

She gave me a glance, innocent like, but I could see she liked me.

"How old are you?"

"I told you the first time we met. Ten. Just today. But age doesn't mean a thing. I have a friend who's eighty-five and he's still around."

"What's your name?"

"You asked me before. Momo."

Then she had to work. She explained about the place, it was what they call a dubbing studio. The people on the screen opened their mouths to speak, but it was the characters in the studio who gave them their voices. It was like mother birds; they put the voices right into their mouths. If the first try was a flop and the voice didn't go in at the right time, they had to do it over. And that's when it was wonderful to watch, because everything went into reverse. The dead came to life and backed into their old place in society. Somebody pressed a button and everything went in the opposite direction. Cars went into reverse, dogs ran backwards, houses that had burned to the ground picked themselves up and put themselves together again before your very eyes. The bullets came out of the body and went back into the guns, the killers left the room and jumped out the window backwards. The water somebody had emptied out climbed back into the glass. The puddle of blood flowed back into the body where it belonged, there wasn't a trace of blood to be seen, and the wound closed right up. A guy who had spat caught the spit in his mouth. Horses galloped backwards and a guy who'd fallen out of the seventh story flew back up again right square into the window. It was a magic world, I've never seen anything sweeter in all my stinking life. For a second I even saw Madame Rosa young and fresh and steady on her pins, and when I turned her back still further, she was even prettier. It brought the tears to my eyes.

I stayed there quite a while because I wasn't urgent anywhere else, and it was beautiful. I liked it especially when the lady on the screen got killed. She stayed dead a while to make people feel bad, and then she got up off the floor as if an invisible hand had picked her up, and backed back to life. The bozo she'd called "my darling, my poor darling" looked like a prize jerk, but that was none of my business. The people saw how much I enjoyed the movie. They told me the whole thing could be run off in reverse from the end to the beginning. One of them with a beard laughed and said: "All the way to the earthly paradise," but added: "unfortunately when it starts up again it's always the same." The blonde told me her name was Nadine and her job was making people speak with a human voice in the movies. I was so happy there was nothing in all the world that I wanted. Think of it. A house burns down and collapses, the fire goes out, the house gets up again. You've got to see it with your own eyes to believe it, because other people's eyes aren't the same thing.

And then I had a real event. I can't say I went back and saw my mother, but I saw myself sitting on the floor, and in front of me there were two legs with boots up to the waist and a leather mini-skirt, and I tried like mad to raise my eyes and see her face, I knew she was my mother, but it was too late, memories can't raise their eyes. I even succeeded in going still further back. I feel two warm arms around me, cradling me, I've got a stomach ache, the person holding me is walking back and forth humming, but I still have a stomach ache. Then I drop a turd, it settles on the floor, the relief makes my stomach ache stop, the warm person kisses me lightly, and I hear, hear, hear . . .

"How do you like it?"

I was sitting in a nice comfortable chair and there was nothing on the screen. The blonde was sitting beside me and they made the light reign.

"Not bad."

Then I had another turn at the bozo getting sprayed with tommy guns, maybe because he was a cashier in a bank or a rival gang, and yelling,

"Don't kill me, don't kill me!" like a dope, because it doesn't do a bit of good, a gunman has his job to do same as everybody else. I like it in a movie when the stiff says, "Very well, gentlemen, do your job," before dying. There's a man who knows the facts of life, because there's really no sense in boring people with appeals to their finer feelings. But the bozo on the screen couldn't catch the right appealing tone and they had to make him back up and start all over. First he'd hold out his hands to stop the bullets, and then he'd yell, "No, no!" and, "Don't kill me, don't kill me!" with the voice of the guy in the studio, who'd be talking into the mike in perfect safety. Then he'd fall and writhe, people always like to see writhing in the movies, and then he'd lie still. The gangsters would give him another burst to make sure he couldn't fight back. And when he was dead beyond repair, the whole contraption went into reverse and the bozo rose up like the hand of God had grabbed him and stood him on his feet to try and use him another time.

Then we saw some other sequences as they call them, and there were some that had to be run back ten times before they came out right. The words went into reverse too and said things backwards, which made mysterious sounds like a language that nobody knows but that's trying maybe to say something.

When there was nothing on the screen, I amused myself imagining Madame Rosa happy, with all her hair from before the war and not even needing to hustle because of the backward-running world.

The blonde patted me on the cheek and I've got

to admit she was nice and it was too damn bad. I thought of her two kids, the ones I'd seen, and well, it was too damn bad.

"You seemed to be having a good time."

"Yeah, it was fun."

"You can come again whenever you like."

"I haven't got much time, I can't promise."

She asked if she could take me out for ice cream and I didn't say no. She liked me too, and when I took hold of her hand to help us walk faster, she smiled. I took chocolate, strawberry and pistachio, but I was sorry afterwards, I should have taken vanilla.

"I like it when you run it backwards. I live with a lady who's going to die soon."

She didn't touch her ice cream, she just looked at me. Her hair was so blond I couldn't help lifting up my hand and touching it. Then I laughed because it was funny.

"Your parents aren't in Paris?"

I didn't know what to say, so I ate some more ice cream, maybe it's what I like best in the whole world.

She didn't insist. It always bugs me when people say what does your daddy do or where's your mummy, it's a topic of conversation I haven't got.

She took a piece of paper and a pen and wrote something and underlined it three times to make sure I wouldn't lose it.

"Here. It's my name and address. Come and see us any time you like. My friend is always there. He takes care of the children."

"A psychiatrist?" I said.

That floored her.

"What makes you say that? It's pediatricians that look after children."

"Only when they're babies. Later it's psychiatrists."

She didn't say anything for a while, just looked at me as if I scared her.

"Who taught you that?"

"My friend Le Mahoute. He knows those things because he's getting disintoxicated. At Marmottan."

She put her hand on mine and leaned close to me.

"Did you say you were ten years old?"

"That's right."

"You know some weird things for a child of ten . . . So it's a promise? You'll come and see us?"

I licked my ice cream. My morale was way down. Good things are even better when your morale is down. I've often noticed that. Chocolate tastes better than usual when you feel like dying.

"You've got somebody already."

She didn't get my meaning. I could tell by the way she looked at me.

I licked my ice cream and looked her straight in the eye with a vengeance.

"I saw you before, just after we met. You went home. You've got two kids already. They're blond like you."

"You followed me?"

"Well . . . yes. You gave me ideas."

I don't know what hit her all of a sudden, but honest to God the way she looked at me was something. You know what I mean. All of a sudden her eyes were four times bigger.

"Listen to me, my little Mohammed . . ."

"Everybody calls me Momo, Mohammed is too much of a mouthful."

"Listen to me, Momo. You have my name and address. Don't lose them. Come and see me whenever you like . . . Where do you live?"

I wasn't going to tell her that. If a chick like her came to our place and found out it was an illegal rest home for whores' children, we'd be disgraced. It wasn't that I really expected her, I knew she had someone already, but when nice people like that see a prostitute's kid, their first thought is procurer, pimp, organized crime, infantile delinquency. We have a very bad reputation with nice people, trust my long experience. They never take us, on account of what Dr. Katz calls the family influence, and for their money a whore is the lowest of the low. And besides, they're afraid of venereal diseases in kids like us that are all hereditary. I didn't like to refuse, so I gave her a phony address. I took her piece of paper and put it in my pocket, you never can tell, but it's no use expecting miracles. She started asking me questions, I didn't say yes and I didn't say no. I had some more ice cream, vanilla this time. Vanilla is the best thing in the world.

"You'll meet my children and we'll all go to the country together . . . We have a house in Fontainebleau . . ."

"Well, good-by."

I jumped up all of a sudden because I hadn't asked her for any favors and beat it with Arthur.

I had fun for a while scaring cars by crossing in front of them at the last minute. People don't like

to run children over, and it gave me a kick to
know I was making them nervous. They'd step on
the brake like a ton of bricks to keep from hurting
you, which isn't much, but it's better than
nothing. I'd have liked to scare them even worse,
but I wasn't up to it yet. I hadn't quite decided
whether to join up with the police or the terrorists,
all in good time, I'd see. Either way, you need an
organized mob, by yourself you're lost, too in-
sulated. I'm not really sold on killing. I'd rather
grow up to be somebody like Victor Hugo. Monsieur Hamil says you can do everything with
words, without killing people and some day when
I have time I'm going to try it. Monsieur Hamil
keeps saying the word is louder than the sword. If
you want my frank opinion, a gunman is what he
is because nobody noticed him when he was little,
so he grew up in the dark. Some kids can't hope to
be noticed because there are too many of them,
they can only attract attention by starving, or they
organize gangs for the same reason. Madame
Rosa says millions of kids starve to death in the
world and some of them even get their pictures
taken. She says the dick is the enemy of the human
race and the only decent person that ever lived was
Jesus, because he didn't come out of one, which is
very exceptional. She says life can be beautiful except that nobody really knows how to make it that
way and meanwhile we've got to live. Monsieur
Hamil also has a lot of good to say about life and
especially Persian carpets.

I felt very important running in between the cars
to scare them, because I can assure you nobody
gets any fun out of running a kid over and I knew

I could get them into real trouble. I had no intention of getting run over just to bug them, but believe me I gave them a good scare. There's a kid I know, we call him Limpy, who got himself run over with the same kind of foolishness. It got him three months of comfort in the hospital, but I can tell you that if he'd lost a leg his father would have sent him out to look for it.

It was dark already and maybe Madame Rosa was starting to worry because I wasn't home yet. So I speeded up fast because I'd been having a good time without Madame Rosa and my conscience was bothering me.

I COULD SEE AT A GLANCE THAT SHE'D deteriorated some more in my absence, especially in the head, which was even farther gone than the rest of her. She often used to say with a smile that life didn't feel at home in her body, and now I saw what she meant. She had pains all over. She hadn't done the marketing for a whole month because of the stairs, and she said if it hadn't been for me and all the worry I gave her she'd have no reason to go on living.

I told her what I'd seen in the studio, the way everything backed up in reverse, but she only sighed and got us our supper. She knew she was deteriorating fast, but she was still a very good cook. The one thing she didn't want for anything in the world was cancer, and there she was in luck, because it was the one thing she didn't have. All the rest of her was so damaged that even her hair had stopped falling out, because the mechanism that made it fall had deteriorated too. In the end I went for Dr. Katz, and he came. He wasn't so very old but he couldn't afford the stairs, because stairs attack the heart. We still had two or three weekly kids, two of them were leaving next day and the third was going to Abidjan, where his mother was retiring to a sex shop. She had celebrated her last trick two days ago after twenty years on the rue Saint-Denis, and she told Madame Rosa that it brought the tears to her eyes and she felt like she'd aged overnight. We helped Dr. Katz up the stairs by supporting him on all sides, and then he sent us out of the room to examine Madame Rosa. When we came back, Madame Rosa was beaming because it wasn't cancer. Dr. Katz was a great doctor, he'd done a good job. And then he looked at us all, I say all, but we were only a handful of leftovers, and I knew I'd soon be all alone. There was an Orléans rumor going around that the Jewess starved us. I don't even remember the names of the three other kids, except a girl called Edith, God knows why, because she wasn't over four.

"Which of you is the oldest?"

I told him it was Momo as usual, because I've never been young enough to keep out of headaches.

"All right, Momo, I'm going to give you a prescription and you'll take it over to the pharmacy."

We went out on the landing, and he looked at me the way they always do to upset you.

"Momo, my boy, Madame Rosa is a very sick woman."

"But you said she didn't have cancer."

"No, she hasn't got that, but frankly, she's in bad shape, very bad."

He told me that Madame Rosa all by herself had enough sicknesses for a whole family and we'd have to put her in the hospital. I remember distinctly his saying something about a ward, which he said was another name for a big room. At the time, I thought it was because all the sicknesses she had wouldn't fit into a small room, but now I believe he said it to throw encouraging colors on the hospital. I didn't understand the names Dr. Katz reeled off with satisfaction, because it was obvious that he'd learned a great deal from examining her. The little I understood was blood pressure, which could attack her at any moment.

"But her main trouble is senility, second childhood if you prefer . . ."

I didn't prefer anything, but it wasn't up to me. He explained that Madame Rosa's arteries had shrunk. Her plumbing was all stopped up and the blood wasn't circulating in the right places.

"Her brain isn't getting the blood and oxygen it needs. Pretty soon she won't be able to think, she'll be like a vegetable. She can drag on for years, she may even have her lucid moments, but . . ."

"But it's not cancer?"

"Definitely not. You can set your mind at rest."

That was good news after all, and I started bawling. I was really glad to hear we'd escaped the worst. I sat down on the stairs and cried like a baby. That's the expression, but in my opinion every age has its own way of crying.

Dr. Katz sat down on the stairs beside me and put his hand on my shoulder. His beard made him look like Monsieur Hamil.

"Don't cry, Momo. It's natural for old people to die. You've got your whole life ahead of you."

Was the bastard trying to scare me, or what? I've always noticed that when old people say,

"You're young, you've got your whole life ahead of you," they smile all over, like it tickled them to think what you're in for.

I stood up. Sure, I knew I had my whole life ahead of me, but I wasn't going to cry myself sick on that account.

I helped Dr. Katz down the stairs and ran back to Madame Rosa with the good news.

"Everything's fine, Madame Rosa, you haven't got cancer. The doctor's positive."

Her smile was enormous, because she has hardly any teeth left. When Madame Rosa smiles, she's not as old and ugly as usual, because her smile is still young and gives her a beauty treatment. She has a picture of when she was fifteen before the German extermination, and looking at it you couldn't believe it would turn out to be Madame Rosa some day. And it was the same thing the other way round. It was hard to imagine Madame Rosa at the age of fifteen. There was no connection between them. At the age of fifteen Madame Rosa had beautiful red hair and a smile like wherever she was going it was full of good things. It gave me a bellyache to see her at fifteen and now in her present state of affairs. Life had done a job on her. That's what. Sometimes I stand at the mirror and try to imagine what I'll be like when life has done a job on me. I do it with my fingers, I tug at my lips and make faces.

So that's how I brought Madame Rosa the best news in her life, that she didn't have cancer.

That evening we opened a bottle of champagne Monsieur N'Da Amédée had given us to celebrate Madame Rosa's not having the worst enemy of the

people, as he said, because Monsieur N'Da
Amédée went in for politics too. She fixed herself
up for the champagne and even Monsieur N'Da
Amédée seemed surprised. Then he left us, but
there was still some in the bottle. I filled Madame
Rosa's glass, we said chin chin, and then I closed
my eyes and threw her into reverse until she was
fifteen like in the picture, and that way I even
managed to kiss her. We drank up the champagne,
I was sitting beside her on a stool, trying to look
cheerful and encourage her.

"Madame Rosa, you'll be going to Normandy
soon. Monsieur N'Da Amédée will give you the
money."

Madame Rosa always said cows were the happiest people in the world and she dreamed of going
to live in Normandy, where they have fresh air. I
felt so weak sitting on that stool and holding her
hand, that I think I'd never wanted so much to be
a cop. Then she asked for her pink kimono, but
we couldn't get her into it, because it was her
floozy kimono and she'd put on too much weight
in the last fifteen years. In my opinion people
don't respect old whores enough instead of per-
secuting them when they're young. If I was able,
I'd devote myself exclusively to old whores,
because the young ones have their procurer and
the old ones haven't got anybody. I'd only take
the ones that are old and ugly and no good for
anything, and I'd be their procurer and take care
of them and make justice reign. I'd be the biggest
cop and procurer in the whole world and with me
around you'd never again see an old whore left to
weep on the seventh floor with no elevator.

"What else did the doctor say? Am I going to die?"

"Not specially. No, Madame Rosa, he didn't especially say you were going to die any more than anyone else."

"What's the matter with me?"

"He didn't count. A little of everything, that's what he said."

"What about my legs?"

"He didn't say anything special about your legs, and you know perfectly well that people don't die with their legs."

"What about my heart?"

"He didn't go into that."

"And what was that he said about vegetables?"

I played innocent.

"Vegetables?"

"I heard him say something about vegetables."

"You'll have to eat vegetables for your health, Madame Rosa. You've always given us vegetables. Sometimes you didn't give us anything else."

Her eyes were full of tears and I went and got some toilet paper to wipe them.

"What will you do without me, Momo?"

"I won't do anything at all, and besides, you're still here."

"You're a pretty little boy, Momo, and that's dangerous. Be very careful, Momo. Promise me you won't peddle your ass."

"I promise."

"Swear it."

"I swear, Madame Rosa. You can set your mind at rest."

"Momo, remember that a man's ass is his most

sacred possession. That's where he keeps his honor. Don't let anybody touch your ass, even for good pay. Even if I die and your ass is all you've got left in the world, don't weaken."

"I know it's a woman's work, Madame Rosa. A man has his dignity to think of."

We stayed like that for an hour hand in hand, and it took away some of her fear.

WHEN MONSIEUR HAMIL HEARD THAT Madame Rosa was sick, he wanted to go up and see her, but with his eighty-five years and no elevator it was outlawed. They'd met thirty years ago when Monsieur Hamil sold carpets and Madame Rosa peddled her ass, it wasn't fair for an elevator to come between them. He wanted to write one of Victor Hugo's poems for her, but his eyes were shot and I had to learn it by heart as coming from Monsieur Hamil. It began with *subhān addaīm lā iazul,* which means that only the Eternal One lasts forever. I climbed up quick to the seventh floor while I still had it and recited it to Madame Rosa, but twice I got stuck and had to go up and down two times six flights to ask Monsieur Hamil for the missing pieces of Victor Hugo.

I said to myself, wouldn't it be a good idea for Monsieur Hamil to marry Madame Rosa, seeing they were the right age and they'd be able to deteriorate together, which is always a pleasure? I mentioned it to Monsieur Hamil, I said we could carry him up on a stretcher for the proposition and then we'd take them out to the country and leave them in a field until death set in. I didn't use those exact words, because that's no way to sell a bill of goods. I only said it was nicer to be two because then you can exchange comments. I also pointed out to Monsieur Hamil that there was nothing to prevent him from living to be a hundred and seven because life seemed to have forgotten him, and seeing as he'd been interested in Madame Rosa once or twice in years gone by, this was a good time to jump on the chance. Since they both needed love, which was impossible at their age, they had all the more reason to join forces. I even brought out the photo of Madame Rosa at the age of fifteen, and Monsieur Hamil admired her through the special glasses he had to see more than other people. He held the picture far away and then he moved it close up, and he must have seen something because first he smiled and second he had tears in his eyes, but not for any special reason, only because he was old. Old people are always dripping.

"You see how beautiful Madame Rosa was before the exterminations. You really ought to marry her. Yes, I know, but you'll always be able to look at the picture when you want to remember her."

"I might have married her fifty years ago if I had known her, my little Mohammed."

"You'd have been disgusted with each other after fifty years. If you do it now, you won't even see each other properly and you won't have time to get disgusted."

He was sitting behind his cup of coffee. He had rested his hand on the Book of Victor Hugo, and he seemed happy, because he was a man who didn't ask for much.

"My little Mohammed, even if I were still

capable of doing such a thing, I couldn't marry a Jewish woman.''

"She's not Jewish or anything else any more, Monsieur Hamil. She's only a woman with pains all over. And you're so old yourself that it's up to Allah to think of you now, not you of Allah. You went to see Him in Mecca, now it's His turn to do something for you. Why not get married now that you're eighty-five and have nothing more to lose?''

"What would we do if we were married?''

"Hell, you're sorry for each other, aren't you? That's what makes people get married.''

"I'm much too old to marry," said Monsieur Hamil, as if he weren't too old for everything.

Madame Rosa was deteriorating so bad I was afraid to look at her. The other kids had been taken away and when a mother came to see about boarding her kid she couldn't help noticing what a wreck she was and the deal was off. The worst of it was that Madame Rosa laid the rouge on thicker and thicker, and sometimes she made goo-goo eyes and luscious lips like she was still on the sidewalk. That was too much, I didn't want to see it. I'd go down in the street and knock around all day and Madame Rosa would be left all alone making goo-goo eyes at the air with her scarlet red lips and her little simpers. Sometimes I'd sit on the sidewalk and run the world backwards like in the dubbing studio, but even further. People would step out of doors and I'd make them go back in backwards, or I'd stand in the street and shoo the cars away. Nothing and nobody could come anywhere near me.

LUCKILY WE HAD NEIGHBORS TO HELP us. I've told you about Madame Lola, who lived on the fifth floor and worked as a transvestite in the Bois de Boulogne because she had a car. Before going to work, she'd often come up and give us a hand. She was only thirty-five and still had plenty of conquests to look forward to. She'd bring us chocolates, smoked salmon and champagne because they're expensive, and that's why people who peddle their ass never put any money aside. Just then there was an Orléans rumor about the North African workers having cholera that they'd brought back from Mecca, and the first thing Madame Lola always did was to wash her hands. Cholera gave her the creeps because it came from dirt and wasn't hygienic. I've never had cholera myself, but I don't think it can be as rotten as Madame Lola said, it's just a sickness and that's that. It never asked to be cholera, it was born that way.

Madame Lola drove her car around the Bois de Boulogne all night. She said she was the only Senegalese in the business and she was very popular, because when she opened up she had beautiful tits and a dick at the same time. She fed those tits on hormones like chickens. She was so hefty because of her past as a boxer that she could hold a table up in the air by one leg, but that's not what people paid her for. I liked her a lot because she wasn't like anybody else. I saw pretty soon that she took an interest in me to give herself the kid she couldn't have in her line of business, because she wasn't equipped for it. She wore a blond wig and breasts, which are very much in demand in women, and she fed them hormones every day and she wiggled when she walked on her high heels and made fruity gestures to draw customers, but she really wasn't like anybody else, so you felt you could trust her. I couldn't see why people are always classified according to their ass and why it's supposed to be so important, when really it can't hurt you one way or the other. I flirted with her a little because we needed her bad, she slipped me money and cooked for us, tasting the sauce with gestures and looks of pleasure, and strutting around on her high heels with her earrings swinging. She told us that when she was young in Senegal she'd knocked out Kid Govella in three rounds but she'd always been unhappy as a man. I'd say to her: "Madame Lola, you're not like anybody else." That pleased her and she'd say: "Yes, my little Momo, I'm straight out of a dream," and that was the truth, she was like the blue clown or Arthur my unbrella, who were very different too. "You'll see, my little Momo, when you're big that there are outward marks of distinction that don't mean a thing, such as balls, which are only an accident of nature." Madame Rosa was sitting in her armchair and asked her to watch what she said because I was still a child. Yes, she

was really okay because she was absolutely like
nothing in nature and never drew a mean breath.
When she was getting ready to go out at night with
her blond wig, her high heels and her earrings, her
beautiful black face with its souvenirs of the ring,
her white sweater which was good for the breasts,
a pink scarf around her neck because of the
Adam's apple, which is very unpopular in transvestites, her skirt with the slit in one side and the
garters, it was really too good to be true.
Sometimes she'd disappear for a day or two to
Saint-Lazare and come back exhausted with her
makeup every which way. Then she'd go to bed
with a sleeping pill, because it's not true that you
get used to everything in the end. One time the
police came to her place looking for drugs but they
didn't find any, some jealous girl friends had slan-
dered her. I'm speaking now of the days when
Madame Rosa could talk and her head was all in
one piece except once in a while when she'd break
off in the middle and look straight ahead with her
mouth open like she didn't know who she was or
where she was or what she was doing there. Dr.
Katz used to call it a state of stupor. She got it
much worse than anybody else, and it came back
regularly, but her Jewish carp was still very good.
Madame Lola came up every day to see how she
was getting along, and when the Bois de Boulogne
was going strong she gave us money. She was
highly respected in the neighborhood and anybody
who took liberties got a poke in the jaw. I don't
know what would have become of us on our
seventh floor if it hadn't been for the six other
floors that had tenants who weren't out to hurt

each other. They'd never reported Madame Rosa to the police when she had as many as ten little sons of bitches raising hell on the stairs.

There was even one Frenchman on the third floor, who behaved like this wasn't his own country at all. He was a tall gaunt man with a cane, and he lived so quietly that nobody noticed him. He heard that Madame Rosa was deteriorating and one day he climbed the four flights from him to us and knocked on the door. He came in and bowed to Madame Rosa. "Madame, my respects." So saying, he sat down with his hat on his knees, as straight as a curtain rod with his head in the air, and took an envelope out of his pocket with a stamp on it and his name written out in so many words.

"My name is Louis Charmette, as the address on this letter indicates. You are welcome to see for yourself. It's from my daughter who writes me once a month."

He showed us the letter with his name written on it, as if to prove he still had one.

"Formerly of the French Railways, administrative staff, now retired. Having just heard that you were ill after twenty years in the same building, I wished to pay my respects."

I've told you that Madame Rosa, in addition to her sicknesses, had lived a lot, which gave her the cold sweats. They got even worse when things happened that she understood less and less, which is always the case when you get old and they accumulate. So this Frenchman who'd taken the trouble to climb four flights of stairs to pay his respects pretty near finished her. She took it to mean she was going to die and this was the official representative, which was all the more natural because he was formally dressed in a black suit, collar and tie. I don't think Madame Rosa wanted to live, but she didn't want to die either, I don't think it mattered much to her either way, it was just a question of habit. If you ask me, there are better things to do.

This Monsieur Charmette was very grave and important, sitting so straight and motionless, and Madame Rosa was terrified. They had a long silence between them, and when that was over they couldn't think of anything to say. If you want my honest opinion, this Monsieur Charmette had come up because he was alone too and he thought maybe they could go into partnership. When you get to a certain age, fewer and fewer people come to see you, except if you have children who obey the law of nature. I think they frightened each other and they exchanged looks that seemed to say: after you, no, if you please, after you. Monsieur Charmette was older than Madame Rosa but he was thin while she overflowed in all directions and there was much more of her to be sick. It's always harder for an old woman, who's been Jewish all her life in addition, than for an employee of the French Railways.

She was sitting in her armchair, holding a fan she'd kept from her past, when gentlemen had given her little presents, and she was so thunderstruck she didn't know what to say. Monsieur Charmette looked her straight in the eye with his hat on his knees and his black suit like he'd come to take her away, and she was in such a cold sweat that her head was trembling. You'll have to admit it's a crazy idea to think Death can come in and sit down with his hat on his knees and look you in the eye, meaning your time has come. It was plain as day to me that he was only a Frenchman who didn't know any more French people and had jumped at the chance to make his existence known when the news that Madame Rosa wouldn't be coming down any more penetrated public opinion as far as Monsieur Keibali's Tunisian grocery store, which was the crossroads of all the news.

This Monsieur Charmette's face was already shady, especially around the eyes, which are the first to sink into their hollows and start living all by themselves with a look of why, by what right, what's happening to me? I remember him well, the way he sat facing Madame Rosa as stiff as a curtain rod, prevented from bending his back by the laws of rheumatism, which increases with age especially when the nights are cool, as is often the case out of season. He had heard in the grocery store that Madame Rosa hadn't long to live, seeing that all her principal parts were affected, so he must have thought that a woman in her condition was more likely to understand him than somebody who was still in good working order, and there he was. Madame Rosa was in a panic, because this was her first visit ever from a French Catholic that sat up straight and didn't say a word. They kept up the silence for a while and then another while. Then finally Monsieur Charmette opened up a little and started talking very severely about all he'd done for the French Railways over the years, which you'll agree was quite a lot to take for an old Jewess in an advanced state. They were both afraid, because it isn't true that Nature always knows best. Nature doesn't know or care what it does or to who, sometimes it's the birds and the flowers and sometimes it's an old Jewish woman on the seventh floor who can't get down the stairs any more. I felt sorry for this Monsieur Charmette because you could see he had nothing and nobody either, in spite of his Social Security. In my opinion, it's mostly the stark necessities that people haven't got.

Old people aren't to blame if they're always attacked in the end, and I'm really not so crazy about the laws of nature.

It was something listening to Monsieur Charmette talking about trains, stations and timetables, like he thought there was still a chance of escaping if he took the right train at the right time and made the right connections, when he knew perfectly well that he'd come to the last stop and there was nothing for him to do but get out.

They went on like that for quite some time, and I was worried about Madame Rosa because I could see she was completely flummoxed by such an official visit, like he'd come to pay her the last honors.

I opened the box of chocolates Madame Lola had given us, but Monsieur Charmette wouldn't touch them, because his organs counterindicated sugar. He finally went back down to his third floor and his visit did no good at all. Madame Rosa saw that people were getting nicer and nicer to her, and that's always a bad sign.

MADAME ROSA'S ABSENCES WERE getting longer and longer, and sometimes she didn't feel anything for hours on end. I thought of the sign Monsieur Reza the shoemaker put up saying to apply somewhere else in case of absence, but I could never find out who to apply to, because some people catch the cholera even in Mecca. I'd sit on the stool beside her, take her hand, and wait for her to come back.

Madame Lola helped us as much as she could. She'd come back from the Bois de Boulogne all worn out from working so hard at her specialty, and sometimes she'd sleep until five in the afternoon. Then in the evening she'd come up and give us a hand. We still had boarders now and then but not enough to live on and Madame Lola said the prostitutional profession was dying out because of the free competition. The ones who do it for nothing aren't persecuted by the police, who are only interested in the ones that are worth something. We had a case of blackmail when a procurer who was nothing but a common pimp threatened to report a whore's kid to the Public Welfare, with loss of paternity rights for prostitution if she refused to go to a whorehouse in Dakar, and we kept the kid for ten days—his

name of all things was Jules—but then Monsieur
N'Da Amédée took the matter in hand and it all
got straightened out. Madame Lola cleaned the
house and helped Madame Rosa to keep herself
clean. I'm not here to throw bouquets at her, but
I've never known a Senegalese that could have
been a better mother than Madame Lola, it's
really a shame that Nature was against it, which
was an injustice to her and put the kibosh on a
whole brood of happy children. She wasn't even
allowed to adopt any, because transvestites are too
different and that's something that society never
forgives. Sometimes it almost broke Madame
Lola's heart.

I can assure you that the whole house was
affected by the news that Madame Rosa was going
to die at the propitious moment, when all her
organs would get together for that express purpose. The four Zaoum brothers were movers, the
strongest men in the neighborhood for pianos and
heavy furniture, and I always admired them
because I'd have liked to be four myself. They
came up and told us they'd be glad to carry
Madame Rosa down and back again any time she
felt like taking a few steps outside. One Sunday,
which is a day when nobody moves furniture, they
picked up Madame Rosa and carried her down
like a piano, and set her up in their car, and we
drove out to the Marne to breathe the fresh air.
Her head was in one piece that day and she even
started making plans for the future, because she
didn't want a religious funeral. At first I thought
the Jewess was afraid of God and figured she
could keep out of His clutches by getting herself

buried without religion. It wasn't that at all. She wasn't afraid of God, but she said it was too late, what was done was done, and there was no point in His coming around to apologize to her. I believe that when Madame Rosa's head was in one piece, she wanted to die for keeps and not have another trip to take afterwards.

On the way back the Zaoum brothers took her on a little tour, Les Halles, rue Saint-Denis, rue de Fourcy, rue Blondel, rue de la Truanderie and so on, and she was really moved, especially on the rue de Provence when she saw the little hotel where she'd been young and able to climb the stairs forty times a day. She told us it gave her pleasure to see the sidewalks and places where she'd worked, it made her feel she'd carried out her contract in full. She smiled, I could see it had picked up her morale, and then she started talking about the good old days, which were the happiest time of her life, so she said. When she'd quit at the age of fifty and then some, she still had regular customers, but in her opinion it wasn't esthetic at that age, and that's when she'd decided to reconvert. We stopped for a drink on the rue Frochot, and Madame Rosa ate a piece of cake. Then we went home. The Zaoum brothers carried her up to the seventh floor as easy as rolling off a log, and she was so delighted with her outing that it seemed to have taken several months off her age.

When we got back, Moïse had come to see us and he was sitting outside the door. I told him hello and left him with Madame Rosa, who was in top form. I went down to the café to see a pal who'd promised me a real leather jacket that came

from genuine American stocks, but he wasn't
there. I stayed a while with Monsieur Hamil, who
was in good health. He was sitting over his empty
coffee cup, smiling peacefully at the opposite wall.

"How's it going, Monsieur Hamil?"

"*Bonjour,* my little Victor, I'm glad to hear
you."

"One of these days they'll invent glasses for
everything, and you'll be able to see again, Monsieur Hamil."

"One must trust in God."

"Some day there will be wonderful glasses like
we've never had before, and you'll really be able
to see, Monsieur Hamil."

"Well, my little Victor, glory be to God, for it is
He who has suffered me to live so long."

"Monsieur Hamil, my name isn't Victor. It's
Mohammed. Victor is your other friend."

He seemed surprised.

"Yes, of course, my little Mohammed . . . *Tawa
kkaltu'ala al-Hayy elladri lā iamūt* . . . I have put
my trust in the living God who never dies . . .
What was it I called you, my little Victor?"

There he goes again.

"You called me Victor."

"How could I do such a thing? I beg your pardon."

"Oh, it's nothing, nothing at all. One name is as
good as another, it doesn't matter. How have you
been since yesterday?"

He seemed to be thinking hard. I saw he was
trying to remember, but all his days were exactly
alike since he'd stopped selling carpets from
morning till night, so everything was white against

white in his head. He kept his right hand on a little worn Book that Victor Hugo had written in, and the Book must have really been used to feeling that hand, like blind people sometimes when you help them to cross the street.

"Since yesterday? Is that what you want to know?"

"Yesterday or today, Monsieur Hamil, it doesn't matter. It's just time that passes."

"Well, today I've been here all day, my little Victor . . ."

I looked at the Book, but I had nothing to say. They'd been together so many years.

"Some day I'll write a real book myself, Monsieur Hamil. With everything in it. Which is Monsieur Victor Hugo's best book?"

Monsieur Hamil looked far into the distance and smiled. His hand moved over the Book, as if to caress it. His fingers trembled.

"Don't ask me too many questions, my little . . ."

"Mohammed."

"Don't ask me too many questions. I'm a little tired today."

I picked up the Book. Monsieur Hamil felt me take it and I could see he was worried. I looked at the title and gave it back to him. I put his hand on it.

"Here, Monsieur Hamil, here it is. You can feel it."

I saw his fingers touching the Book.

"You're not like other children, my little Victor. I've always known that."

"Some day I'll write my own *Misérables,* Monsieur Hamil. Will there be someone to take you home later?''

''*Insh'Allah*. There's sure to be, because I believe in God, my little Victor.''

He had this Victor on the brain, and I was fed up.

''Tell me a story, Monsieur Hamil. Tell me about your big trip to Nice when you were fifteen.''

He looked surprised.

''Me? A big trip to Nice?''

''Yes, when you were very young.''

''I don't remember. I don't remember at all.''

''All right, then I'll tell *you*. Nice is an oasis on the seashore, with mimosa forests and palm trees and Russian princes and English lords and they have battles with flowers. There are clowns dancing in the streets and confetti falling from the sky, enough for everybody. Someday when I'm young I'm going to Nice myself.''

''What? When you're young? Are you old? How old are you, little . . . You are little Mohammed, aren't you?''

''Nobody knows. They don't know my age either. I'm not dated. Madame Rosa says I'll never be my own age because I'm different and that's all I'll ever be good for. Do you remember Madame Rosa? She's going to die soon.''

But Monsieur Hamil was lost inside, because sometimes life keeps people alive but doesn't care much what becomes of them. There's a lady in the house across the street, Madame Halaoui, who used to come at closing time and take him home and put him to bed, because she didn't have anybody either. I don't even know if they cared about each other or if it was only to keep from being alone. She had a peanut stand on the Boulevard Barbès, and so did her father in his lifetime. So I said:

"Monsieur Hamil! Monsieur Hamil!" Just to remind him there was still someone who loved him and knew his name, and that he had one.

I stayed with him quite a while, letting the time pass, the kind of time that passes slowly and isn't French. Monsieur Hamil had often told me that Time comes slowly from the desert with its camel caravans and isn't in any hurry because it's carrying eternity on its back. But Time is always nicer to talk about than to see on the face of an old man who's sinking a little more every day, and if you want my honest opinion Time is just a thief.

The owner of the café, you're sure to know him because it's Monsieur Driss, came over to see how we were getting along. Monsieur Hamil needed to piss now and then, and somebody had to take him to the can before the hurry was too much for him. But I wouldn't want you to think that Monsieur Hamil was irresponsible and worthless. Old people may not be what they used to be, but they're worth as much as anyone else. They have feelings same as you and me, and sometimes they suffer even more because they're too old to defend themselves. Their worst enemy is Nature, which can be a very ugly customer and kills them by slow torture. And France is even worse than Nature, because it's against the law to put old people out of their misery when Nature is choking them by degrees and their eyes are popping out of their heads. That's the way it was with Monsieur Hamil, who was perfectly capable of getting a lot older and maybe dying at the age of a hundred and ten with the world championship in his buttonhole. He was still perfectly responsible and said "pee-pee" when he needed to, before it happened, and Monsieur Driss took him by the elbow and personally guided him to the can. When a man is very old and it looks like he'll be removed soon, the Arabs treat him respectfully; it gives them good marks in God's account books, which is no sneezing matter. All the same it was sad for Monsieur Hamil needing to be escorted to the can and I left them there and then, because in my opinion sadness is a good thing to keep away from.

I WAS CLIMBING THE STAIRS WHEN
I heard Moïse crying, and I ran the rest of the way
because I thought maybe something had happened
to Madame Rosa. I went in and at first breath I
couldn't believe my eyes. To tell you the truth, I
closed them; I thought maybe I'd open them
better next time.

Madame Rosa's auto tour of all the streets she'd
walked had affected her like a miracle. Her whole
past came back to her. She was naked in the
middle of the room, dressing to go out and peddle
her ass like in the old days. Well, I haven't seen
much in my life, so maybe I'm not entitled to say
what's scary and what isn't, but you can take my
word for it that Madame Rosa, mother-naked in
leather boots, with black lace panties around her
neck, because she'd gotten her arms and legs
mixed up, and tits that defy the imagination lying
flat on her belly, is something you won't see
anywhere else even if it exists. To make it worse,
she was trying to wiggle her ass like in a sex shop,
and that ass was bigger than humanly possible.
Siyyid! . . . I mumbled a prayer, for the first time
in my life I think, that prayer for the *mahbūl*,
the nuts and loonies, but she went on wriggling
with a naughty little smile and a twat like I

wouldn't wish on my worst enemy.

I knew all this was the effect of the recapitulative shock she'd gotten from revisiting the scenes of her past happiness, but sometimes understanding is no help at all, on the contrary. She was so densely made up that the rest of her looked even more naked, and the way she screwed up her lips into rosebuds made you want to throw up. Moïse was in the corner, bawling his head off. I just said, "Madame Rosa, Madame Rosa." Then I beat it down the stairs and out into the street. It wasn't to get away, that wasn't possible, I just didn't want to be there.

I ran pretty far and when that made me feel better I sat down in a doorway in the dark, behind the garbage cans that were waiting to be taken away. I didn't cry, because what was the use. I was so ashamed that I shut my eyes and buried my face in my knees. I stayed there a while and then I called a cop. He was the biggest strongest cop you can imagine, a million times braver than all the rest put together, with even more armed security forces. He had tanks and cannons at his beck and call, so I stopped worrying, because I knew he'd take care of my self-defense. He put his all-powerful arm around me paternally and asked me if I had any wounds. I told him yes, I had, but I didn't see the point of going to the hospital. He stayed there for quite some time with his hand on my shoulder, and I had a feeling that he'd take care of everything and be like a father to me. Pretty soon I decided that my best bet would be to go and live in the place where things were different. When Monsieur Hamil was still with us, he used to say that poets ran the other world, and all of a sudden I smiled, because I remembered how he'd called me Victor and I thought maybe he was God and was promising me something. Then I saw white and pink birds that you could blow up, with a string on the end that you could grab and fly away, far far away, and then I dropped off asleep.

I had a good sleep and then I went to the café on the rue Bisson, which is mostly black on account of the three African lodging houses next door. In Africa life is completely different; they've got tribes, and when you belong to a tribe it's like having a big family. Monsieur Aboua was there, I didn't tell you about him before because I can't tell you everything at once, and that's why I'm mentioning him now. He can't even speak French, so somebody else has to speak for him or you wouldn't know he was there. I stayed there quite a while with Monsieur Aboua. He's from Ivory Coast. We held hands and laughed and enjoyed ourselves. I was ten and he was twenty; he got a kick out of the difference and so did I. Monsieur Soko, the owner, told me not to stay too long, he didn't want trouble with the Society for the Protection of Minors. A ten-year-old kid can be a source of complications on account of dope, because that's the first thing people think of when they see a kid. Minors are wonderfully protected in France, and when there's nobody to look after them the government throws them in jail for safekeeping.

Monsieur Soko has children that he left in Ivory, because he's got more women there than here. I knew I wasn't supposed to loiter without my parents in an establishment for public intoxication, but I just didn't want to go home. The state I'd left Madame Rosa in still gave me goose flesh, just to think of it. It was bad enough to see her dying little by little for no reason, but mothernaked with that whorehouse smile, waiting for the customers, all two hundred and twenty pounds of her including an ass that defied human measurement, was a situation that called for laws to put an end to her suffering. Everybody's been talking lately about protecting the laws of nature, but if you ask me, the laws of nature are for the birds. I couldn't spend my life in a bar, so I went back home. All the way up the stairs I said to myself that maybe Madame Rosa had died in the meantime and wouldn't be suffering any more.

I opened the door slowly because I was afraid of scaring myself. The first thing I saw was Madame Rosa standing in the middle of the room with a little suitcase next to her. You'd have thought she was on a Métro platform, waiting for the train. One quick look at her face and I saw she was too happy to be where she was, in fact she was miles away. Her eyes were off in the distance under a hat that wasn't the least bit becoming, which was too much to expect, but at least it hid part of her face. She was smiling as if she'd just heard some good news. She had on a blue dress with daisies and she'd rummaged her old whore's handbag out of the cupboard which she kept for sentimental reasons, I knew it well, it still had rubbers in it, and she was looking through the walls like she was taking the train for good and always.

"What are you doing, Madame Rosa?"

"They're coming to get me. They'll attend to everything. They said to wait here. They're coming in trucks and they'll take us to the Velodrome with our strict necessities."

"Who they?"

"The French police."

I didn't get it. Moïse was in the other room, making signs to me, touching his head. Madame Rosa had her old professional handbag in her hand and her suitcase beside her. She looked nervous, like she was afraid of being late.

"They gave us half an hour. Just one suitcase, they said. They're putting us on a train and sending us to Germany. I won't have one thing to worry about. They'll attend to everything. They promised not to hurt us and said we'd be roomed and boarded and laundered."

I didn't know what to say. I thought maybe they'd started shipping Jews to Germany again because the Arabs didn't want them around. When Madame Rosa's head was in one piece, she'd often told me how Monsieur Hitler had set up a charnel home for Jews in Germany and they'd all been absorbed except their shoes and clothing, teeth and bones, which were taken away to avoid waste. But I couldn't see why the Germans always had to bear the brunt, why they should have to be rigging up homes for the Jews again, because what about all the other countries, by rights it was their turn to make a few sacrifices. Madame Rosa never got sick of reminding me that she'd been young once herself. Okay, I knew all that because I'd been living with a Jewish woman and with Jews that kind of stuff always comes out

in the end, but I couldn't see why the French
police should take an interest in Madame Rosa,
who was old and ugly and had nothing whatsoever
to recommend her. I knew she was falling into
second childhood on account of her mental
derangement; her senility was coming out, just as
Dr. Katz had warned me. She must have thought
she was young, same as before when she'd put on
her floozy clothes, and there she was with her little
suitcase, happy as a lark because she was just out
of her teens, waiting for the doorbell to take her
back to the Velodrome and the Jewish home in
Germany.

I didn't know what to do, because I didn't want
to cross her, but I knew damn well the French
police weren't coming to make Madame Rosa
young again. I sat down on the floor in a corner
and kept my head down because that way I
couldn't see her. That was all I could do for her.
Luckily she came back all of a sudden and she was
the most surprised of all to see herself standing
there with her suitcase, her hat, her blue dress with
the daisies, and her old handbag full of memories,
but I thought I'd better not tell her what had happened, I could see she'd forgotten all about it. It
was an attack of amnesty. Dr. Katz had warned
me she'd have more and more of them, until one
day she'd blank out for good, after which she
could go on living for years and years in a state of
vegetation.

"What happened, Momo? Why am I standing
here with my suitcase, like I was going away?"

"You've been dreaming, Madame Rosa. It
never hurt anybody to dream a little."

She gave me a suspicious look.

"Momo, I want you to tell me the truth."

"I swear it's the truth, Madame Rosa. You haven't got cancer. Dr. Katz is positive. There's nothing to worry about."

That seemed to relieve her a little; cancer was a good thing not to have.

"Why am I standing here with no idea what I've been doing and why? What's wrong with me, Momo?"

She sat down on the bed and began to cry. I went and sat down beside her and took her by the hand, she liked that. She smiled and smoothed my hair to make me look nicer.

"Madame Rosa, it's just life, that's all. You can live to a ripe old age with it."

She thought a moment.

"I don't understand. I had my menopause long ago, I worked all through it. Are you sure it's not a brain tumor, Momo? They're fatal too when they're malignant."

"He didn't say anything about fatal or not fatal. He only told me it was your age and not a word about amnesty or anything."

"Do you mean amnesia?"

Moïse, who had no business there, began to bawl, which was all I needed.

"Moïse, what is it? Is he lying? Is he hiding something? What's he crying about?"

"Holy Christmas, Madame Rosa, Jews always cry among themselves, you know that. Hell, they've got a wall for that very purpose."

"Could it be cerebral sclerosis?"

I was good and sick of it. I was so fed up I had a good mind to get Le Mahoute to give me a family-size fix and tell them all to go to hell.

"Momo! Are you sure it's not cerebral sclerosis? That's fatal."

"Can you think of anything that isn't, Madame Rosa? That kind of talk makes me want to take a good shit. On my mother's grave."

"Don't say such things. Your poor mother is . . . well, maybe she's alive."

"I wouldn't wish that on her, Madame Rosa. Even if she's alive, she's still my mother."

She gave me a funny look and then she smiled.

"You're growing up, my little Momo. You're not a child any more. Some day . . ."

She was going to tell me something, but she stopped herself.

"Some day what?"

For a second she looked guilty.

"Some day you'll be fourteen. Then fifteen. And you won't want me around any more."

"Don't talk bullshit, Madame Rosa. I won't run out on you, it's not my style."

That relieved her, and she went and changed. She threw on her Japanese kimono and put perfume behind her ears. I don't know why she always put the perfume behind her ears, maybe so nobody would see it. Then I helped her to sit down in her armchair, because it was hard for her to bend. Considering what was wrong with her, she was in good shape. She seemed sad and anxious and I was glad, because that was her normal condition. She even cried a little, which proved she was really all right.

"You're a big boy now, Momo. So now you understand."

I don't need to tell you how not true that was. I didn't understand anything, but I wasn't going to argue, this wasn't the time . . .

"You're a big boy, so listen . . ."

At that point she skipped a few cylinders and for a while she conked out like an old jalopy with engine trouble. But seeing she wasn't a jalopy, I held her hand and waited for her to come to. Once after I'd been to see him three times in a row Dr. Katz told me about an American who'd lived in a comma like a vegetable for seventeen years in the hospital; they'd extended him by medical methods, and when he died he held the world record. All the world champions are in America. Dr. Katz told me there was nothing more to be done with her, but that with good hospital care she could go on for years.

The trouble was that Madame Rosa had no Social Security because she was clandestine. Since that raid by the French police when she was still young and useful as I've had the honor, she hadn't wanted to figure in anybody's records. I know a pile of Jews in Belleville with identity cards and all sorts of telltale documents, but Madame Rosa wasn't willing to take the risk, because once you've got official papers that prove you exist, they know who you are and that's something they never forgive. Madame Rosa hadn't one drop of patriotism in her veins, she didn't care if you were a North African or an Arab, a Malian or a Jew, because she had no principles. She used to say there's some good in every nationality, and that's why there are gentlemen known as historians who study them on purpose and write books. In short, Madame Rosa wasn't registered anywhere, and she had false papers proving she had no connection with herself. So we couldn't expect the Social Security to pay her medical expenses.

But Dr. Katz put me to rest by telling me that if you take a body that's still alive but too far gone to fend for itself to the hospital, they can't throw it out, because where would it go?

I looked at Madame Rosa and thought about all that while her head was off somewhere else. It was what they call accelerated senile dementia with stops and starts culminating in finality. For simplicity's sake, a person in that condition is said to be dotty; that comes from the word dotage, which is medical. I patted her hand to encourage her to come back. I'd never loved her more, because she was ugly and old, and pretty soon she wouldn't even be a human being any more.

I didn't know what to do. We had no money and I wasn't old enough to escape the anti-minor law. I looked older than ten, and I knew I was popular with the whores who didn't have anybody else, but the police were down on the pimps and I was scared of the Yugoslavs too, because they hate competition and that makes them even more dangerous than the Corsicans.

Moïse tried to cheer me up by telling me he was a hundred per cent satisfied with the Jewish family that had taken him over, and if I tried I could find somebody too. He promised to come back every day and give me a hand. Madame Rosa had to be wiped, because she couldn't do it herself. Even in the days when her head was free and clear, she'd had problems in that department. Her ass was so big that her hand couldn't reach to the right place. She hated being wiped because of her feminine delicacy, but what could you do? Moïse came around like he'd promised, and that's when we had the national catastrophe that I had the honor and that aged me from one minute to the next.

ONE DAY THE OLDEST ZAOUM brother brought us flour, oil and meat to make meatballs with. A lot of people had started showing their good side since Madame Rosa's deterioration. I marked that day with a red letter, because it's a nice expression.

Madame Rosa was feeling better with ups and downs. Sometimes she closed up completely and sometimes she stayed open. One of these days I'm going to thank all the tenants who helped us, like Monsieur Waloumba, who ate fire on the Boulevard Saint-Michel to get pedestrians interested in his case. He came up and put on a marvelous act for Madame Rosa in the hope of arousing her attention.

Monsieur Waloumba is a black from the Cameroons, who came to Paris to sweep it. He'd left all his wives and children at home for economic reasons. When it came to fire eating, he was Olympic class, and he devoted his overtime hours to his art. The police had it in for him because he provoked encumbrances, but he had a working permit as a fire eater. When I saw Madame Rosa sitting there with a vacant look and her mouth open, drooling in the other world, I ran for Monsieur Waloumba, who shared a legal domicile with eight other members of his tribe in a room on the sixth floor. If he was home, he'd come quick with his lighted torch and start spitting fire for Madame Rosa. It wasn't just to entertain a sick person aggravated by melancholy, but also to give her a shock treatment, because Dr. Katz said patients were often improved by suddenly having the electricity turned on to them, which is another form of the same treatment. Monsieur Waloumba agreed. He said old people often recover their memory if somebody frightens them and he'd even cured a deaf-mute that way in Africa. Sometimes it makes old people even sadder when they're put in the hospital for good. Dr. Katz says old age is merciless and after sixty-five or seventy nobody gives a damn about you.

So we spent hours and hours trying to scare Madame Rosa and curdle her blood. Monsieur Waloumba is terrifying when he eats fire and the flames come out of his mouth and shoot up to the ceiling, but Madame Rosa was having one of her slow periods that they call lethargy, when you couldn't care less and nothing makes the slightest impression. Monsieur Waloumba vomited flames for a whole half hour and she just sat there in a stupor with glazed eyes like as if she'd been a statue that nothing could faze, because it's made of wood or stone for that express purpose. Then he thought he'd make one last try, and while he was trying Madame Rosa suddenly emerged from her state. When she saw a black man, bare to the waist and spitting fire, she let out a horrible yell. She even tried to escape, and we had to stop her. After that she wouldn't have anything to do with it and absolutely prohibited fire eating on the premises. She didn't know she'd been off her rocker. She thought she'd been taking a little nap and we'd woken her up. We couldn't tell her.

Another time Monsieur Waloumba brought five of his tribal brothers and they danced around Madame Rosa, trying to chase away the evil spirits that attack certain persons whenever they get a moment's free time. Monsieur Waloumba's brothers were well known in Belleville and people asked them to perform this ceremony whenever they had sick people eligible for treatment. Monsieur Driss of the café despised what he called "these practices." He made fun of Monsieur Waloumba and accused him and his tribal brothers of practicing "black market medicine."

Monsieur Waloumba and his crowd came up one evening when Madame Rosa was absent, sitting in her armchair with glassy eyes. They were half naked, decorated in several colors, with their faces painted something awful to scare the demons the African workers bring to France with them. Two of them were sitting on the floor with their hand drums, and the three others started dancing around Madame Rosa in her armchair. Monsieur Waloumba played a musical instrument made especially for the purpose. It went on all night and it was really the best show in Belleville. It didn't help any because that kind of thing doesn't work with Jews. Monsieur Waloumba said it was a question of religion. He thought Madame Rosa's religion put up a fight and that made her unfit to be cured. Which surprised me a lot because in the state Madame Rosa was in it was hard to see where she could find room for religion.

After a while Monsieur Waloumba's brothers got discouraged because in Madame Rosa's condition she didn't notice anything. Monsieur Waloumba explained that their efforts couldn't get in because the evil spirits were blocking all the exits. So we all sat down on the floor around Madame Rosa and took a breather, because there's a lot more black people in Africa than in Belleville, so they can work on their evil spirits in shifts like the Renault factory. Monsieur Waloumba went out for rum and hen's eggs and we feasted Madame Rosa, who kept swiveling her head as if she'd lost her mind and was looking all over for it.

While we were feasting, Monsieur Waloumba told us it was much easier to respect old people and take care of them and ease their sufferings in his country than in a big city like Paris with its thousands of streets, stairways, holes and corners, where they're forgotten and the army can't be called out to look for them because the army only looks for the younger generation. If the army spent its time taking care of old people, it wouldn't be the French Army any more. He told me there were tens of thousands of these nests of old people in the cities, towns and villages, but nobody was giving out the information needed to locate them, and the result was ignorance. An old man or woman in a big and beautiful country like France is a sorry sight, without which people already have trouble enough. Old people are no use for anything, they've lost their public utility, so their youngers just let them live. In Africa everybody belongs to a tribe and the old people are very much in demand because they can do so much for you when they're dead. In France there aren't any tribes on account of self-seeking individualism. Monsieur Waloumba says that France is completely detribalized and that's why young people band together in armed gangs and try to do something about it. Monsieur Waloumba says that young people need tribes, because without them they're like a drop in the ocean, and that drives them crazy. Monsieur Waloumba says everything is getting so big anything under a thousand isn't even worth counting. That's why little old men and women who can't form armed gangs disappear without leaving an address and end their lives in dusty holes. Nobody knows they're there, especially when it's maids' rooms with no elevator and they can't scream to attract attention because they're too weak. Monsieur Waloumba says they should send a lot of manpower over from Africa to wake these old people up at six in the morning and take away the ones that are starting to smell bad, because nobody ever checks to see if they're alive or dead, and it's only when somebody goes to the concierge and reports a bad smell on the stairs that the truth comes to light.

Monsieur Waloumba speaks well and you can always tell that he's the chief. His face is covered with scars. Scars are marks of importance, thanks to which he's highly respected in his tribe and knows what he's talking about. He's still living in Belleville and I'm going to see him one of these days.

He showed me a little trick that could come in

handy for Madame Rosa, how to distinguish a person who's alive from one who's completely dead. He got up from his chair, took a mirror from the washstand and held it in front of Madame Rosa's lips. It clouded over in the place where she'd breathed on it. Without it you couldn't see she was breathing, seeing her weight was too heavy for her lungs to lift. That's how you tell the difference between the living and the other people. Monsieur Waloumba says the first thing that should be done every morning is to see if the people of another age that you find in maids' rooms without elevators are a hundred per cent dead or only stricken with senility. If the mirror clouds over you know they're still breathing and shouldn't be disposed of.

I asked Monsieur Waloumba if we couldn't send Madame Rosa to his tribe in Africa so she could live with other old people and benefit by the same advantages. Monsieur Waloumba laughed his head off, because his teeth are very white, and his brothers of the sanitation tribe laughed too; they talked to each other in their language and then they told me that life isn't so simple, because it requires airplane tickets, money and permits, and it was my duty to take care of Madame Rosa until death do us part. Just then we noticed a glimmer of intelligence on Madame Rosa's face, and Monsieur Waloumba's tribal brothers started dancing around her and beating drums and singing loud enough to wake the dead, which is prohibited after ten o'clock at night for reasons of public order and the sleep of the just, but there aren't very many French people in the building and they're not as furious as they would be anywhere else. Monsieur Waloumba picked up his musical instrument that I can't describe because it's something very special, and Moïse and me joined in too. We all started dancing and yelling in a circle around Madame Rosa to exercise her, because she seemed to be showing signs and needed encouragement. We put the demons to flight and Madame Rosa's intelligence came back, but when she saw all those black men, with green, white, blue and yellow faces dancing around her whooping like Indians to the strains of Monsieur Waloumba's magnificent instrument, she was so scared she began screaming help help and tried to run away, and it wasn't till she recognized Moïse and me that she calmed down and called us sons of bitches and motherfuckers, which proved that her brain was back to normal. We all congratulated ourselves and Monsieur Waloumba first of all. They all stayed a while for refreshments, and Madame Rosa saw they hadn't come to beat an old woman in the Métro and snatch her pocketbook. She still wasn't completely right in the upper story, and she thanked Monsieur Waloumba in Jewish, which is called Yiddish in that language, but it didn't matter because Monsieur Waloumba was a good man.

After they left, Moïse and me undressed Madame Rosa from top to toe and cleaned her up with Clorox, because she'd soiled herself during her absence. Then we powdered her ass with baby powder and put her back in her armchair, where she liked to reign. She asked for a mirror and did her face over. She knew she had these blackouts but she did her best to take them with Jewish good humor, saying that when she was vacant she had no worries, which was something. Moïse went out to the store with our last savings and she cooked a little something without any mistakes or anything, and nobody would have suspected that she'd been out cold two hours ago. It was what Dr. Katz, in medical language, calls a suspended sentence. Then she went and sat down because exertions were hard on her. She sent Moïse to the kitchen to wash the dishes. Then she ventilated herself for a while with her Japanese fan and meditated in her kimono.

"Come here, Momo."

"Now what? You're not going to conk out again?"

"No, I hope not. But if this goes on they'll put me in the hospital. I don't want to go. I'm sixty-seven . . ."

"Sixty-nine."

"All right, sixty-eight. I'm not as old as I look. So listen to me, Momo. I don't want to go to the hospital. They'll torture me."

"Madame Rosa, don't talk bullshit. France hasn't ever tortured anybody. This isn't Algeria."

"They're going to keep me alive by force, Momo. That's what they always do in the hospital. They've got laws that tell them to. I don't want to live any longer than necessary, and it's not necessary already. Even for Jews there's a limit. They'll torture me to keep me from dying. They've got a shebang called the Medical Association just for that. They put you through hell to the bitter end and they won't give you permission to die because then you'd be a privileged class and it wouldn't be democratic. I had a friend who wasn't even Jewish but he had no arms and legs on account of an accident, and they tortured him in the hospital for ten years to study his circulation. Momo, I don't want to live just for the sake of medical science. I know I'm losing my mind and I don't want to hang on for years in a comma just to make the doctors happy. So if you hear any Orléans rumors about sending me to the hospital, I want you to get your friends to give me the right kind of injection and leave my remains in the country. In a clump of bushes, anywhere. I once spent ten days in the country after the war, and I've never breathed so much. It's better than the city for asthma. For thirty-five years I gave my ass to the customers, and I'm not giving it to the doctors now. Promise?"

"I promise, Madame Rosa."

"Khaïrem?"

"Khaïrem."

Which means "I swear" in their language, as I've had the honor.

I'd have promised Madame Rosa anything to make her happy, because even when a person is old a little happiness can come in handy, but just then the doorbell rang, and that's when the national catastrophe happened that I haven't had a chance to tell you about yet and it gave me a big joy because aside from everything else it aged me by several years from one minute to the next.

THE BELL RANG, I OPENED THE DOOR, and what do I see but a little guy even sadder than most, with a long droopy nose and eyes like you see wherever you go but even more scared. He was ashly pale and he sweated a lot and breathed fast with his hand on his heart, not because of sentiments but because there's nothing worse than the heart for climbing stairs. His coat collar was turned up, and he had no hair like a lot of bald people. He was holding his hat in his hand like as if to prove he had one. I don't know where he was out of, but I'd never seen anybody so nervous. He gave me a panicky look and I paid him back in kind, because a single glance at this character was all I needed to tell me that something was going to blow sky-high and fall back down on me from all sides.

"Madame Rosa. Is this the place?"

You've always got to be careful in situations like that, because persons unknown don't climb six flights to pat you on the back.

I played dumb, which is normal at my age.

"Who?"

"Madame Rosa."

I stopped to think. You've always got to gain time in those situations.

"No. It's not me."

146

He sighed, he took out his handkerchief, he wiped his forehead, and then he did it again in reverse.

"I'm a sick man," he said. "Just out of the hospital after eleven years. I've climbed six flights of stairs without the doctor's permission. I've come to see my son before I die, it's my legal right, even the savages have a law to that effect. All I want is to sit down a minute and get my breath and see my son. Is he here? I entrusted my son to Madame Rosa eleven years ago. I have a receipt."

He rummaged in his coat pocket and gave me a scrap of paper so filthy you couldn't believe it. I was able to read it thanks to Monsieur Hamil, to whom I owe everything. I'd be nothing without him. *Received from Monsieur Kadir Youssef five hundred francs in advance for little Mohammed, of Moslem condition, October 7, 1956.* It gave me a shock all right, but this was 1970, I did a quick subtraction, 1956 was fourteen years ago, so it couldn't be me. Madame Rosa must have had whole truckloads of Mohammeds, that's one thing there's no shortage of in Belleville.

"Wait, I'll go and see."

I went and told Madame Rosa that a guy with an ugly mug was there to see if he had a son. She was scared pink.

"But my goodness, Momo, there's only you and Moïse."

"Then it's got to be Moïse," I said. Call it self-defense. It was him or me.

Moïse was asleep in the other room. Of all the big sleepers I've ever known he was the sleepingest.

"Maybe he wants to blackmail the mother," said Madame Rosa. "Never mind, we'll see. It takes more than a pimp to scare me. He can't prove a thing. My false papers are above suspicion. Bring him in. If he starts getting rough, you can notify Monsieur N'Da Amédée."

I brought him in. Madame Rosa's three remaining hairs were in curlers, she had on her makeup and her red Japanese kimono. One look at her and the guy's knees started trembling so bad that he sat right down on the edge of a chair. I could see that Madame Rosa was trembling too, but her tremors were harder to see because she didn't have the strength to hoist her excess weight. All the same her brown eyes are a very pretty color if you don't pay attention to the rest. The visitor was sitting on the edge of his chair with his hat on his knees, facing Madame Rosa, who was reigning in her armchair, and I was standing with my back to the window to keep him from getting a good look at me, because you never know. There was no resemblance at all between him and me, but I have a golden rule of thumb, never to take any chances. Especially because he turned in my direction and examined me as if he were looking for a nose that he'd lost. Nobody breathed a word. We were all so scared that none of us wanted to start in. I even went and got Moïse, because this character had a receipt in due and proper form; so naturally we had to produce the goods.

"You wished to speak to me, monsieur?"

"Eleven years ago, madame, I entrusted my son to you . . ." It must have been hard for him to talk, because he kept gasping for breath. "I couldn't communicate with you any sooner, because I was shut up in the hospital. I didn't even have your name and address, because they took everything away from me when they locked me up. My poor wife, as you are well aware, died a tragic death. Your receipt was in her brother's possession. They let me out this morning, I recovered the receipt, and here I am. My name is Kadir Youssef, and I've come to see my son Mohammed.''

Madame Rosa's head was all in one piece that day. That's what saved us.

I could see she'd turned pale, but you had to know her, because with her makeup on she was all red and blue. She put on her glasses, which were always more becoming to her than nothing, and looked at the receipt.

"What was the name again?"

The guy almost burst into tears.

"Madame, I'm a sick man."

"Who isn't, who isn't?" said Madame Rosa piously. She even raised her eyes to heaven like in thanksgiving.

"Madame, my name is Kadir Youssef, Youyou to the hospital nurses. Male nurses, may I add. I was psychiatric for eleven years after the tragedy in the newspapers, for which I was absolutely irresponsible."

I suddenly remembered all the times Madame Rosa had asked Dr. Katz if he thought I was psychiatric. Or hereditary. Oh well, what did I care? It wasn't me. I was ten years old, not fourteen.

"What was your son's name again?"

"Mohammed."

The way Madame Rosa's eyes stabbed into him I was even more scared than before.

"And the mother's name? Do you remember that by any chance?"

I thought the guy would drop dead. He turned green, his jaw sagged, his knees jiggled and the tears came out of his eyes.

"Madame, you know perfectly well that I was irresponsible. I was diagnosed and certified as such. If my hand did that, I had no part in it. It's true they didn't find syphilis, even though the nurses claim that all Arabs are syphilitic. I did it in a moment of madness, God keep her soul. I have become very pious, I pray for her soul every hour. Considering her occupation, she needs it. I acted in a fit of jealousy. Think of it. Up to twenty tricks a day. In the end I got jealous and killed her. I admit it. But I'm not responsible. I was certified by the best French doctors. I didn't remember a thing afterwards. I loved her madly. I couldn't live without her."

Madame Rosa smiled. A fiendish smile. I'd never seen anything like it. No, I can't describe it. It froze my guts.

"Naturally you couldn't live without her, Monsieur Kadir. Ayisha had been bringing you in a thousand francs a day for years. You killed her to make her bring you more."

The guy let out a sharp scream. Then he began to cry. It was the first time I'd seen an Arab cry except myself. It had so little to do with me that I even felt sorry for him. All of a sudden Madame Rosa softened. She'd cut the guy's balls and that cheered her up. I guess it made her feel that she was still a woman.

"And otherwise, Monsieur Kadir? Are you well?"

The guy wiped his face with his fist. He didn't even have the strength to reach for his handkerchief. It was too far away.

"Pretty well, Madame Rosa. I'm going to die soon. My heart."

"Mazel tov," said Madame Rosa kindly, which means congratulations in Yiddish.

"Thank you, Madame Rosa. I would like to see my son if you please."

"You owe me three years' board, Monsieur Kadir. For eleven years you didn't give me a single sign of life."

The guy jumped sky-high in his chair.

"Sign of life, sign of life, sign of life!" he screamed, with his eyes raised to heaven, where all of us are expected. "Sign of life!"

Every time he said those words he jumped in his chair as if somebody had kicked him in the ass without the slightest respect.

"Sign of life! No! You must be joking!"

"I never joke," said Madame Rosa. "You dropped your son like a lump of shit, as the saying goes."

"But I didn't have your name and address. Ayisha's uncle had the receipt in Brazil . . . I was locked up. I got out this morning. I went to see his daughter-in-law in Kremlin-Bicêtre, they're all dead except the mother, who inherited the property and vaguely remembered something. The receipt was pinned to a photograph of Ayisha as

mother and child! Sign of life! What do you
mean, sign of life?"

"Money," said Madame Rosa sensibly.

"Where do you expect me to find money,
madame?"

"That's a question I don't wish to go into,"
said Madame Rosa, ventilating her face with her
Japanese fan.

Monsieur Kadir Youssef was swallowing so
much air that his Adam's apple shot up and down
like an express elevator.

"Madame, when we entrusted our son to your
care I was in full possession of my resources. I had
three women working on the rue Saint-Denis, one
of whom I loved tenderly. I could afford to give
my son a good education. I even had an official
name, Youssef Kadir, well known to the police.
Yes, madame, *well known to the police*. A
newspaper once printed those very words: Youssef
Kadir, well known to the police . . . *Well* known,
madame, not *badly* known. Then I was overcome
with irresponsibility and plunged myself into . . ."

The guy cried like an old Jewish woman.

"You had no right to drop your son like a lump
of shit without paying," said Madame Rosa
severely, and ventilated her face with her Japanese
fan.

The only part of all this that interested me was
to know if this Mohammed was me or not. If it
was me, it meant that I wasn't ten but fourteen,
and that was important, because if I was fourteen
I wasn't nearly so much of a kid and that's the
best thing that can happen to anybody. Moïse,
who was standing by the door listening, wasn't

worrying either, because if this character's name was Kadir and Youssef, there was very little chance of his being a Jew. Mind you, I'm not saying it's good luck to be Jewish, because they have their problems too.

"Madame, I don't know if you're taking that tone with me or if I'm mistaken and my psychiatric state leads me to imagine things, but I was cut off from the outside world for eleven years, which put me in a position of physical impossibility. I have a medical certificate to prove it . . ."

He rummaged nervously in his pockets. He was the kind of guy that isn't sure of anything and it was perfectly possible that he didn't have the psychiatric paper he thought he had because imagining things was just what they'd locked him up for. Psychiatric cases are people who are always being told they haven't got what they've got and don't see what they see, and in the end it drives them crazy. Actually he found a real paper in his pocket and tried to give it to Madame Rosa.

"Don't come around me," said Madame Rosa, "with documents that prove something." And she spat three times: "Ptoo, ptoo, ptoo," which is the compulsory, Jewish way of warding off bad luck.

"But I'm all right now," said Monsieur Youssef Kadir, and he looked at us all to make sure it was true.

"Please proceed," said Madame Rosa, because there was nothing else to say.

But he wasn't the least bit all right to judge by the way his eyes went looking for help. It's always the eyes that need it most.

"I couldn't send you the money because after declaring me irresponsible they locked me up. I think it was my poor wife's uncle who sent you that money before he died. I'm a victim of fate. Naturally I wouldn't have committed a crime if my condition had been without danger to society. I can't bring Ayisha back to life, but I want to embrace my son before I die and beg him to forgive me and pray to God for me."

He was beginning to give me a pain with his fatherly sentiments and demands. First of all, he absolutely didn't have the right mug to be my father, who must have been the real thing, a big strong son of a bitch and not a weeping willow. And besides, if my mother hustled on the rue Saint-Denis with a very good turnover as he himself said, how could anybody claim me as a father? I was a child of father unknown, guaranteed genuine by the law of large numbers. I was glad to know my mother's name was Ayisha. I can't think of a prettier name.

"They took excellent care of me," said Monsieur Youssef Kadir. "I don't have violent fits any more, I'm cured on that side. But I haven't long to live. My heart. It can't stand emotion. The doctors let me out for sentimental reasons to see my son, to embrace him and ask him to forgive me . . ."

Hell. A long-playing record.

". . . and ask him to pray for me."

He turned toward me and looked at me in a terrible fright because of the emotion the answer was sure to give him.

"Is it him?"

But Madame Rosa had all her wits and then some. She ventilated herself, while looking at Monsieur Youssef Kadir with advance relish.

She ventilated herself some more in silence. Then she turned to Moise.

"Moïse. Say *bonjour* to your papa."

"B'jour, p'pa," said Moïse cheerfully, because he knew he wasn't an Arab and had nothing to hide.

Monsieur Youssef Kadir turned even paler than possible.

"Beg your pardon. What's that? Did you say Moïse?"

"Of course I said Moïse. Why not?"

The guy stood up. He looked to be under the influence of something very strong.

"Moïse," he said, "is a Jewish name. I'm absolutely sure of it, madame. Moïse is not a good Moslem name. Well, there may be some, but not in my family. I entrusted a Mohammed to you, madame, not a Moïse. I can't have a Jewish son, madame. My health doesn't permit it."

Moïse and I looked at each other and managed to keep a straight face.

Madame Rosa seemed surprised. Then she seemed even more surprised. Then she ventilated herself. Then we had an enormous silence in which all sorts of things happened. The guy was still standing on his feet but trembling from top to toe.

Madame Rosa went "tss, tss" with her tongue and shook her head. "Are you sure?"

"Sure of what, madame? I'm sure of absolutely nothing, we were not put into this world to be sure. I have a weak heart. I'm only saying one little thing, one very little thing, but there I insist. Eleven years ago I entrusted a son to you, a Moslem son aged three and named Mohammed. You gave me a receipt for a Moslem son, Mohammed Kadir. I am a Moslem, my son was a Moslem, his mother was a Moslem. Nay more. I gave you an Arab son in due and proper form and I expect you to give me back an Arab son. I absolutely don't want a Jewish son, madame. I don't want one, period. My health won't permit it. I gave you a Mohammed Kadir, not a Moïse Kadir, madame, I don't want to go insane again. I have nothing against the Jews, madame, God forgive them. But I'm an Arab, a good Moslem, and I had a son of the same faith. Mohammed, Arab, Moslem. I entrusted him to you in good condition, and I expect you to give him back in the same condition. Permit me to inform you that emotions of this kind are more than I can bear. I have suffered persecution all my life, I have medical documents to prove it, informing all whom it may concern that I am suffering from persecution."

"Then you're sure you're not a Jew?" Madame Rosa asked hopefully.

Several nervous spasms passed over Monsieur Kadir Youssef's features.

"Madame, I can be persecuted without being a Jew. You have no monopoly. The Jewish monopoly is finished, madame. Other peoples have as much right as the Jews to be persecuted. I want my son Mohammed Kadir back in the same Arab and Moslem condition described in the receipt you gave me eleven years ago. I don't want a Jewish son under any pretext whatsoever. I have enough trouble as it is.''

"All right, all right, don't get excited,'' said Madame Rosa. ''Maybe there's been a mistake,'' because she could see that the guy was shaken to the foundations and you couldn't help feeling sorry when you think of what the Arabs and the Jews have been through together since the beginning of time.

"There has definitely been a mistake. Oh, my God!'' said Monsieur Youssef Kadir, and he had to sit down because his legs made him.

"Momo, let me see those papers,'' said Madame Rosa.

I hauled the big family suitcase out from under the bed. Seeing as I'd rummaged through it lots of times in search of my mother, nobody was better acquainted with the mess that reigned in that suitcase. When Madame Rosa took in a whore's kid, she put him down on a scrap of paper that nobody could make head or tail of, because our motto was discretion and our customers could sleep soundly. They could be sure nobody would denounce them as prostitute mothers with loss of paternity rights. If some pimp thought he could ship them to Abidjan by blackmailing them with their kid, he'd never be able to locate a kid in Madame Rosa's files even if he'd studied law and engineering.

I gave Madame Rosa the whole pile of papers. She licked her fingers and started searching through her eyeglasses.

"Ah, here it is!'' she cried triumphantly, putting her finger on it. "October 7, 1956. Yes, yes.

That day I took delivery of two boys, the one being a Moslem, the other a Jew . . ."

She stopped to think and her face lit up with comprehension.

"Ah!" she cried with visible pleasure. "That explains it all. I must have gotten the right religion wrong."

"What?" said Monsieur Youssef Kadir, looking interested to the marrow of his bones. "What!"

"I must have brought up Mohammed as Moïse and Moïse as Mohammed," said Madame Rosa. "I took them in the same day and I got them mixed up. Little Moïse, the right one, is now in a good Moslem family in Marseilles, where they're extremely pleased with him. And your little Mohammed, whom you see before you, has been brought up as a Jew. Bar mitzvah and all. He has always eaten kosher, you needn't worry."

"What! Always eaten kosher?" Monsieur Kadir Youssef squeaked. He was so prostrated all along the line that he didn't even have the strength to get up. "My son Mohammed has always eaten kosher? He's had his bar mitzvah? My son Mohammed has been turned into a Jew?"

"It's only an identical mistake," said Madame Rosa. "Identity can make mistakes, you know, it's not foolproof. A three-year-old child has very little identity, you know, even when circumcised. I got the circumcisions mixed and brought up your little Mohammed as a good little Jew, you needn't worry. And when you leave your kid for eleven years without going to see him, you have no call for surprise if he turns into a Jew . . ."

"But I couldn't! It was a clinical impossibility!"

"Oh well, he was an Arab, now he's slightly Jewish, but he's still your little boy," said Madame Rosa with a sweet family smile.

The guy stood up. Indignation gave him strength and he stood up.

"I want my Arab son!" he shouted. "I don't want a Jewish son!"

"But it's the same one," said Madame Rosa encouragingly.

"He's not the same at all! He's been baptized!"

"Ptoo ptoo ptoo!" Madame Rosa spat. Even she had her limits. "He has not been baptized! God forbid. Moïse is a good little Jew, Moïse, aren't you a good little Jew?"

"Yes, Madame Rosa," said Moïse with pleasure, because religion didn't mean a thing to him one way or the other.

Monsieur Youssef Kadir stood up and looked at us with horror in his eyes. Then he started stamping his foot. It was a sort of scalp dance.

"I want my son back in his original condition. I want my son in good Arab condition and not in bad Jewish condition."

"Arab and Jew are all the same to us here," said Madame Rosa. "If you want your son, you'll have to take him as is. First you murder the child's mother, then you get yourself certified psychiatric, and then you make a *tsimmes* because your son has been raised as a Jew without malice aforethought! Moïse, go and kiss your father even if it kills him. He's your father after all."

"Nothing to it," I said to Moïse. You see, I'd

just found out I was four years older and that was the best news I'd had in all my life.

Moïse took a step toward Monsieur Youssef Kadir, and Monsieur Youssef Kadir said something terrible for a man who didn't know he was right.

"He is not my son!" he cried, bursting with tragedy.

He stood up, he took a step toward the door, and the next thing he did was independent of his will. Instead of leaving as he intended, he said *ah!* and then *oh!,* put his hand on the left side of his chest where the heart is known to be and fell to the floor like a man who has nothing more to say.

"Now, what's the matter with him?" Madame Rosa asked, ventilating herself with her Japanese fan, because there was nothing else to do. "What's the matter with him? We'd better see."

We didn't know if he was dead or if it was only temporary, because he showed no indication. We waited, but he refused to move. Madame Rosa began to panic because the last thing we needed was the police, who never stop once they start. She told me to run and get somebody quick, but I could see he was completely dead because of the perfect calm that comes over the faces of people who have nothing more to worry about. I pinched Monsieur Youssef Kadir here and there and I held the mirror to his lips, but there was no problem. Moïse naturally beat it quick, that was his specialty, and I ran for the Zaoum brothers and told them we had a dead man and they should put him on the stairs to show he hadn't died in our place. They came up and put him on the third-floor landing in front of Monsieur Charmette's door, because he was certified French, and could afford it.

Then I went back and sat down beside Monsieur Youssef Kadir and stayed there a while, irregardless that there was nothing more we could do for each other.

His nose was much longer than mine, but noses always get longer as life goes on.

I looked in his pockets to see if I could find some souvenir, but there was only a pack of cigarettes, blue Gauloises. There was still one left and I smoked it sitting beside him, because he'd smoked all the rest, and it gave me a kind of feeling to smoke the last one.

I even cried a little. It gave me pleasure, as if I'd had somebody my own and lost him. Then I heard the police and I beat it upstairs, because I didn't want any trouble.

MADAME ROSA WAS STILL IN A PANIC and I was glad to see her in that state instead of the other. We'd been lucky. Some days her head was in one piece for only a few hours, and Monsieur Kadir Youssef had picked just the right time.

I was still completely flabbergasted at the thought of aging four years from one minute to the next, and I didn't know which kind of a face to put on it, I even looked at myself in the mirror. It was the biggest event of my life, a revolution. I didn't know where I was at, like always happens when you're not the same any more. I knew I couldn't think the same as before, but for the moment I preferred not to think at all.

"My goodness!" said Madame Rosa. We tried not to talk about what had just happened, because we didn't want one thing to lead to another. I sat down on a stool at her feet and took her hand with gratitude for what she had done to keep me with her. We were all we had in the world, so that much at least was saved. In my opinion, when you live with somebody that's very ugly, you end up loving this person for that very reason. In my opinion, people who are really horrible looking are always in need of love, and that's why they're the best possible bet. But come to think back, Madame

Rosa wasn't that ugly by a long shot, she had beautiful brown eyes like a Jewish dog, but it was no good thinking of her as a woman, because from that angle she was a loser.

"Has it made you sad, Momo?"

"Oh no, Madame Rosa. I'm glad to be fourteen."

"It's better this way. Besides, a father with a psychiatric history wouldn't be right for you, because it can be hereditary."

"That's a fact, Madame Rosa. I'm lucky."

"And another thing. Ayisha, as you know, had an enormous turnover. How are we to know which of all those turnovers was the actual father? She conceived you on the run, that woman never stopped working for the time it takes to draw breath."

Later on I went downstairs and bought her a piece of chocolate cake from Monsieur Driss, which she ate.

Her head stayed free and clear for several days. It was what Dr. Katz called a suspended sentence. The Zaoum brothers toted Dr. Katz up the stairs twice a week on one of their backs to estimate the damage; he couldn't have taken the six flights himself. Because you mustn't forget that Madame Rosa had other organs in addition to her head and needed vigilance all over. I never wanted to be there while he was computing. I'd go down in the street and wait for him.

One day the Nigger came by. We called him the Nigger for little known reasons, maybe to distinguish him from the other blacks in the neighborhood, because there's always got to be one who pays for the rest. He's the skinniest of the lot, he wears a derby hat, and he's fifteen years old, at least five of which all by himself. Originally he had parents, but they unloaded him on an uncle, who passed him on to his sister-in-law, who passed him on to some do-gooder, and the end was a vicious circle, so vicious that nobody knew where it started. But he didn't take junk, because he had a grudge against society and he wanted to keep it in good condition. He was known in the neighborhood as a message carrier, because he was cheaper than a phone call. Some days he'd carry as many as a hundred messages, and he even had a pad of his own. He saw I wasn't on top of my form and invited me to play Baby Foot with him in the bar on the rue Bisson where they had one. He asked me what I was fixing to do if Madame Rosa kicked off. I told him I had someone else in mind, but he knew damn well I was bluffing. I told him I'd just put on four years from one minute to the next, and he congratulated me. We chewed the fat for a while about how to make a living if you were fourteen or fifteen with nobody to help you. He knew some addresses but he said if you go in for ass peddling, you better be sure you like it, because it makes you throw up if you don't. He'd never done it himself, because he said it was a woman's business. We smoked a cigarette together and we played Baby Foot, but the Nigger had his errands and I'm not the kind that fastens on to people.

When I went upstairs, Dr. Katz was still there. He was trying to persuade Madame Rosa to go to the hospital. A few other people were there too,

the oldest Zaoum brother, Monsieur Waloumba,
who was off duty just then, and five friends from
the black lodging house, because the approach of
death is a mark of importance and people respect
a person more. Dr. Katz lied like nobody's
business to foment good humor because morale
makes a difference too.

"Ah, here comes little Momo to hear the latest
news. Well, the news is first-rate. Still no cancer,
you have my word for it, ha ha ha!"

Everybody smiled, especially Monsieur Waloumba, who was a keen psychologist, and
Madame Rosa was happy too, because she'd succeeded in something after all, in not having
cancer, I mean.

"But we have our difficult moments, because
sometimes our poor head doesn't get the proper
circulation, and considering that our heart and
kidneys aren't what they used to be, it might be
better if we went to the hospital for a while, where
we'd be lodged in a big beautiful room and
everything would come out all right in the end."

It gave me the shivers to listen to Dr. Katz.
Everybody in the neighborhood knew there was
no way of getting abortioned at the hospital. They
thought nothing of keeping you alive by force as
long as you had enough meat on your bones to
stick a needle into. Medicine has to have the last
word and fight to the last ditch to prevent God's
will from being done. Madame Rosa was wearing
her blue dress and her embroidered shawl, which
was valuable, and it made her happy to be an ob-
ject of interest. Monsieur Waloumba started
playing his musical instrument because it was one

of those painful moments so to speak, when nobody can do anything for anybody. I smiled too, but I wanted to die inside. Sometimes I get a feeling that life isn't what it ought to be, far from it, trust my long experience. Then they all left, one by one in silence, because there are times when there's nothing more to say. Monsieur Waloumba played a few more notes for us, and they followed him down the stairs.

The two of us were left alone as I wouldn't wish on my worst enemy.

"Did you hear that, Momo? Now it's the hospital. What will become of you?"

I started to whistle a little tune. That was the most I could say.

I turned to her, I was going to say any old thing, some kind of optimistic nonsense, but there I had a stroke of luck, because at that exact moment her head backed up again and she was absent for two days and three nights without knowing it. But her heart kept beating and she was still officially alive.

I didn't dare to call Dr. Katz or even the neighbors, because I was sure they'd separate us this time. I stayed there beside her as long as possible. I didn't even go out to piss or eat. I wanted to be there when she got back, so's to be the first thing she saw. I put my hand on her heart and felt it in spite of all the pounds that came between us. The Nigger came up because he hadn't seen me around lately, and he stood there smoking a cigarette and looking at Madame Rosa. Then he rummaged in his pocket and gave me a printed card that said: *Heavy objects removed. Tel. 278 78 78.*

Then he patted me on the back and went away.

THE SECOND DAY I RAN OUT AND GOT Madame Lola and she came up with her loudest shouting pop records. She said they'd wake the dead, but nothing came of it. She'd turned into the vegetable Dr. Katz had anticipated from the start and Madame Lola was so upset at seeing her friend in such a state that she didn't go to the Bois de Boulogne the first night, though she lost a pretty penny by it. That Senegalese was really okay, and I'll go to see him or her one of these days.

We had to leave Madame Rosa in her armchair. In spite of her years in the ring, Madame Lola couldn't lift her.

The saddest part of it when somebody takes leave of his head is that you don't know how long it will last. Dr. Katz had told me the world's record was held by an American with seventeen years and a little more, but for that you need private nursing and special machines that feed you drop by drop. It was awful to think that maybe Madame Rosa would get to be world's champion, because she'd already had as much as she could take and if there was anything that left her cold it was breaking records.

I haven't known many people as nice as

Madame Lola. She'd always wanted to have children, but as I've informed you she wasn't equipped for it, like most transvestites, who in that respect are outlawed by the laws of nature. She promised to take care of me, she made me sit on her lap and sang me a Senegalese lullaby. They have lullabies in France too, but I'd never heard one because I'd never been a baby, I'd always had other things to worry about. I said I was sorry I couldn't play dolls with her, because I was fourteen and it wouldn't seem right. Then she went down to dress for her work, and Monsieur Waloumba got his tribe to mount guard over Madame Rosa. They even cooked a whole sheep and sat on the floor around her eating it like a picnic. It was nice, it gave me a feeling of being in the country.

We tried to feed Madame Rosa by chewing her meat for her, but she'd sit there with pieces half in and half out of her mouth, looking at hundreds of things she couldn't see with her good Jewish eyes. It didn't matter, she had enough fat on her to feed herself and Monsieur Waloumba's whole tribe for that matter, but those days are over, they don't eat people any more. Seeing they were all in a good humor from drinking palm liquor, they finally started dancing and playing music around Madame Rosa. The neighbors didn't complain because they're not the complaining kind and every last one of them had something the matter with his papers. Monsieur Waloumba made Madame Rosa drink a little palm liquor that you can buy on the rue Bisson from Monsieur Somgo, who also sells cola nuts, which are indispensable too, especially for weddings. It seems palm liquor was good for Madame Rosa because it rises to the head and opens the passages, but this time it pulled a blank except to make her a little red. Monsieur Waloumba thought Death was around the corner and the main thing was to play the tom-tom a lot to keep him away, because Death was scared stiff of tom-toms for reasons of his own. Tom-toms are little drums they beat with their hands, and it went on all night.

The second day I was sure Madame Rosa was out to break the world record and we wouldn't be able to avoid the hospital, where they'd do their damnedest. I went out and walked around, thinking of God and that kind of stuff, because I wanted to get still further away from it all.

I ended up on the rue de Ponthieu, and I went to that studio with the machine that makes the world go backwards. Besides, I wanted to see the pretty blond chick that smelled so nice and I've told you about; you know, her name was Nadine or something. Maybe I wasn't being exactly loyal to Madame Rosa, but what could I do? I was in such a state of deprivation that I'd almost forgotten the four extra years I'd gained. It was like I was still ten, I hadn't built up the force of habit yet.

All right, if I told you she was there in that room waiting for me, you wouldn't believe it. I'm not the kind of guy anybody waits for. But she was there all right, and I could almost taste the taste of the vanilla ice cream she'd treated me to.

She hadn't seen me come in, she was saying words of love into the mike, and those things keep you busy. A woman was on the screen, but it was

my chick who supplied the voice. It's hard to explain, because it's technical.

I waited in the corner. I was feeling so low I'd
have cried if I hadn't been four years older. Even
as it was, I had to keep hold of myself. The light
went on and the chick saw me. It was still kind of
dim, but right away she knew who I was. And then
the floodgates opened, I couldn't hold them back.

"Mohammed!"

She ran over to me and put her arms around me.
The others looked at me, because it's an Arab
name.

"Mohammed! What's wrong? Why are you
crying? Mohammed!"

I wasn't so crazy about her calling me Mohammed, because it sounds much further away than
Momo, but what could I do?

"Mohammed! Say something! What's wrong?"

You can imagine if it was easy to tell her. I
didn't even know where to begin. I took a big
swallow.

"It's . . . it's nothing, nothing at all."

"Look. I've finished my work. Come home
with me. You'll tell me all about it."

She picked up her raincoat and we left in her
car. Now and then she turned to me and smiled.
She smelled so good I could hardly believe it. She
could see I wasn't on top of my form, I even had
the gulps. She didn't say anything, because what
was the use, but now and then she'd put her hand
on my cheek thanks to a red light, which always
feels good in such cases. We arrived in front of her
address on the rue Saint-Honoré, and she drove
her car into the courtyard.

Up at her place there was a guy I didn't know. He was tall with long hair and glasses, and he shook hands with me but didn't say anything, as if it were perfectly natural. He was kind of young, no more than two or three times older than me. I looked around expecting the two blond kids they had already to come out and tell me they didn't need me, but there was only a dog and he wasn't unfriendly either.

They started talking English between themselves in a language I didn't know, and then I was served tea and sandwiches that were mighty good and I really had a feast. They let me eat as if there were nothing else to do and then the guy said a few words to me. He asked if I was feeling better and I tried to say something but there was such heaps and heaps that I couldn't even breathe properly and I got the gulps and asthma like Madame Rosa, because asthma is contagious.

I sat there as dumb as a Jewish carp with the gulps for half an hour and I heard the guy say I was in a state of shock, which gave me pleasure, because it seemed to interest them. After a while I got up and said I had to go home seeing there was an elderly person in a state of deprivation who needed me, but this Nadine went to the kitchen and came back with some vanilla ice cream that was the most beautiful thing I've ever eaten in my whole lousy life, and that's the honest truth.

After that we started talking, because I was feeling good. When I told them the elderly person was an old Jewish woman in a state of deprivation who was out to break the world record and what Dr. Katz told me about vegetables, they pronounced words I'd heard before such as senility and cerebral sclerosis, and I was happy because I was talking about Madame Rosa and that always gives me pleasure. I told them Madame Rosa was an ex-whore who'd come back from being deported to the Jewish homes in Germany and had opened a clandestine rest home for the children of whores who could be blackmailed with loss of paternity rights for illicit prostitution and have to hide their kids because neighbors are usually bastards capable of reporting you to the Public Welfare. I don't know why it suddenly did me good to be talking to them. I was seated comfortably in an armchair, the guy even offered me a cigarette and lit it with his lighter, and listened to me as if I was important. I wouldn't want to brag, but I could see I was making an impression. I was so wound up I couldn't stop because I wanted to get everything off my chest, but naturally that was impossible, because I'm not Monsieur Victor Hugo and I haven't got the equipment yet. It came out on all sides at once, because I kept starting at the ragged end, with Madame Rosa in a state of deprivation and my father killing my mother in a psychiatric fit, but I have to admit that I've never known where it all began and where it ends, because in my opinion it just keeps going on. My mother's name was Ayisha, she peddled her ass and did as many as twenty tricks a day until she was killed in a fit of madness but it's not at all certain that I'm hereditary, because Monsieur Kadir Youssef couldn't swear he was my father. Madame Nadine's guy was called Ramon and he told me he was some kind of a doctor and he didn't set much store by heredity and I shouldn't count on it. He lit my cigarette again with his lighter and told me that whores' children were better off than others in a way, because they were free to choose any father they liked without obligation. He told me that accidents of birth often turned out fine in the end and produced good people. Sure, I said, okay, okay, if you're here you're here, it's not like Madame Nadine's projection room, where you can throw the whole works into reverse and crawl back inside your mother, and the worst of it is that it's illegal to abortion old people like Madame Rosa when they're fed up. It did me a lot of good talking to those two, because once I'd gotten my story off my chest I felt like it hadn't happened so much. I kind of liked this guy Ramon's face. He fiddled a lot with his pipe while I was talking, but I could see it was me he was interested in. My only worry was that Nadine would leave us alone, because without her the sympathy wouldn't have been the same. She had a smile on her face that was all for me. When I told them how I struck fourteen from one minute to the next when I'd been only ten the day before, it really stopped them. I did my best to excite their interest even more and make them feel I was giving them their money's worth.

"The other day my father came around, he wanted to take me back; he'd deposited me with Madame Rosa before killing my mother and getting himself certified psychiatric. He had other floozies working for him, but he killed my mother because she was his favorite. So when they let him out, he came around and wanted me back, but

Madame Rosa wouldn't have it. She thought it wouldn't be good for me to have a psychiatric father, because sometimes it's hereditary. So she told him Moïse was his son, and Moïse is a Jew. The Arabs have Moïses too, but they're not Jewish. Well, I don't have to tell you, this Monsieur Youssef Kadir was a Moslem Arab, and when Madame Rosa offered him a Jewish son, he bursted several blood vessels and it killed him . . ."

Dr. Ramon was listening too, but it was mostly Madame Nadine that gave me pleasure.

". . . Madame Rosa is the ugliest, loneliest, miserablest woman I ever saw. Luckily she's got me because no one else would want her. What I don't understand is why some people have everything, they're ugly, old, poor and sick, and others have nothing at all. It's not fair. I have a friend that's chief of the whole police force; he has the strongest security forces in the whole world, he's the biggest cop you can imagine. He's so strong there's nothing he can't do, he's the king. When we walk in the street together, he puts his arm over my shoulder like to show that he's practically my father. When I was little, a lioness used to come and lick my face, I was only ten at the time and I imagined things. At school they said I was disturbed because they didn't know I was four years older, I wasn't dated yet. That was long before Monsieur Youssef Kadir nominated himself as my father with his receipt to back him up. I learned everything I know from Monsieur Hamil the famous carpet dealer, and now he's blind. Monsieur Hamil carries a Book of Monsieur Vic-

tor Hugo around with him and when I'm big I'm
going to write my own *Misérables*, because that's
what people always write if they have anything to
say. Madame Rosa was afraid I'd erupt into
violence and damage her by cutting her throat
because she thought maybe I was hereditary. But a
whore's kid can never know who his father is and I
for my part will never kill anybody, that's not
what people are for. When I'm big, I'll have all
the security forces under my thumb and I'll never
be afraid. It's too bad we can't turn everything
backwards like in your projection room and throw
the world into reverse so Madame Rosa could be
young and beautiful and a pleasure to behold.
Sometimes I think of going away with a circus
where the clowns are friends of mine, but I can't
tell everybody to go to hell and split as long as
Madame Rosa's alive, because I have to take care
of her . . ."

I was getting more and more hopped up and I
couldn't stop talking because I was afraid that if I
stopped they wouldn't listen to me any more. Dr.
Ramon, for it was he, had a face with eyeglasses
and eyes that looked at you. At one point he even
got up and turned on the tape recorder to help him
listen better and I felt more important than ever, I
couldn't believe it. He had big piles of hair on his
head. Nobody had ever taken an interest in me
before, and imagine being plugged into a tape
recorder. I've never been able to figure out what
you have to do to be considered worthy of interest—gun down a carload of hostages or what?
Take it from me, brother, there's so much
disregard in this world that it's hard to choose,

like rich people on vacation who can't go to the mountains and the seashore at the same time. You've got to decide which kind of disregard you prefer and people always pick the biggest and most expensive, like the Nazis, who cost millions, or Vietnam. So naturally an old Jewish woman on the seventh floor without an elevator isn't likely to be seeded first or even second, far from it. People need millions and millions to feel concerned, and you can't blame them, because little things don't amount to much.

I spread out in my armchair and talked like a king, and the craziest part was that they listened as if they'd never heard anything like it. But it was mostly Dr. Ramon who encouraged me to talk, I had a feeling that the chick didn't want to listen, sometimes she even made motions like she was going to stop her ears. Which struck me as kind of funny, because hell, we can't help living, can we?

Dr. Ramon asked me what I meant by a state of deprivation, and I said it was when you didn't have nothing or nobody. Then he wanted to know how we'd managed to scrape along since the whores had stopped boarding their kids with us, but there I set his mind at rest right away. I told him a man has no more sacred possession than his ass, as I had learned from Madame Rosa before I even knew what it was used for. I assured him that I didn't peddle mine and he needn't worry, and I told him about our friend Madame Lola, who worked as a transvestite in the Bois de Boulogne and helped us a lot. "If everybody was like her," I said, "the world would be a different kettle of fish and there'd be much less misery. She was a boxing champion in Senegal before setting up as a transvestite. She makes enough to raise a family if she didn't have nature against her."

The way they listened I could see they weren't in the habit of living. I told them about the time I'd spent as a procurer on the rue Blanche to make a little pocket money. From time to time Dr. Ramon said something political to Madame Nadine but I didn't quite get it because politics isn't for kids.

God knows what I told them. There was so much on my chest I wanted to go on and on. But I was dog tired and even beginning to see the blue clown who was beckoning to me like he often does when I'm dropping off to sleep. I was afraid they'd see him too and think I was hereditary or something. Anyway I couldn't talk any more. They saw I was exhausted and said I could spend the night there, but I explained that I had to go and take care of Madame Rosa, who was going to die, and then I'd see. They gave me another piece of paper with their name and address. Then Nadine said she'd take me home in the car and the doctor would come with us and take a look at Madame Rosa to see if there was anything he could do for her. I didn't see what he could do for Madame Rosa after everything that had been done for her already, but it was all right with me to be driven home in the car. But then a funny thing happened.

We were just going out when somebody rang the doorbell five times in a row. When Madame Nadine opened, I saw the two kids I'd seen before. It was her kids, they'd just come home from school or some such place, and this was their home, I couldn't deny it. They were blond and dressed like you'd think you were dreaming, in luxury clothes, the kind you can't steal, because they don't display them on the sidewalk, they keep them inside and you have to pass the salesgirl barrier to get to them. They looked at me like a lump of shit. My rags were terrible, I felt it right away. I had a cap that was always standing up in back because I have too much hair and an overcoat that hung down to my heels. When you snatch garmentry, you haven't got time to measure if the stuff is too big or too little, you're in a hurry. They didn't say anything, but we weren't from the same block.

I've never seen kids as blond as those two. And I can swear they hadn't been used much, they were as good as new. We just had nothing in common.

"Come and meet our friend Mohammed," said their mother. She shouldn't have said Mohammed, she should have said Momo. Mohammed in France sounds like "Arab asshole," and when anybody calls me that I get mad. I'm not ashamed of being an Arab, not at all, but Mohammed in France sounds like street sweeper or day laborer. It's not the same thing as "Algerian." Besides, Mohammed sounds idiotic. It's like calling somebody Jesus Christ in France, it makes everybody laugh.

The two kids looked me over. The younger, who seemed about six or seven because the other one must have been about ten, stared at me as if he'd never seen anything like it. Then he asked:

"Why is he dressed like that?"

I wasn't going to act insulted. I knew I wasn't at

home there. But then the other one stared even harder and asked:

"Are you an Arab?"

Hell, I don't let anybody call me an Arab. Besides, it was no use trying. I wasn't jealous or anything, but the job wasn't for me and anyway it was taken, there was nothing I could do. I had a lump in my throat, so I swallowed it and beat it out of the house.

We just weren't from the same block.

I STOPPED OUTSIDE A MOVIE, BUT THIS picture didn't admit minors. It's a laugh when you think of the things minors aren't allowed to see and all the other stuff they are.

The cashier saw me looking at the pictures outside and yelled at me to beat it for the protection of my childhood. The asshole. I was good and sick of protecting my childhood, so I unbuttoned my fly, showed her my pecker and cleared out fast, because it was no time for jokes.

In Montmartre I passed a lot of sex shops, but they're protected too and besides I don't need gadgets to jerk off with when I feel like it. Sex shops are for old men who can't jerk off by themselves any more.

The day when my mother didn't get an abortion was genocide. Madame Rosa always had that word on her lips; she was educated, she'd been to school.

Life isn't for everybody, only for the chosen few.

I didn't stop anywhere else before going home, I only wanted one thing, to sit down beside Madame Rosa, because she and I were the same class of shit.

When I got there, I saw an ambulance in front

of the house. I thought this was it and I didn't have anybody any more, but it wasn't for Madame Rosa, it was for somebody who was dead already. I was so relieved I would have cried if I hadn't been four years older. I'd already started thinking I had nothing left. The body belonged to Monsieur Bouaffa. Monsieur Bouaffa, you know, the one I haven't told you about because there was nothing to say, because he didn't show himself very often. He'd had a heart attack and the oldest Monsieur Zaoum, who was standing outside, told me nobody had noticed he was dead because he never got any mail. I've never been so glad to see anybody dead. I had nothing against him, why should I, I was thinking of Madame Rosa, it was one less headache for her.

I ran upstairs, the door was open, Monsieur Waloumba's friends had gone, but they'd left the light on so Madame Rosa could see herself. She was spread out on her armchair and you can imagine my pleasure when I saw the tears flowing from her eyes, because it proved she was still alive. She was even kind of shaken from inside like when people are sobbing.

"Momo . . . Momo . . . Momo . . ." That's all she could say, but it was enough for me.

I ran and kissed her. She didn't smell good because she'd shat and pissed in her pants by reason of her condition. I kissed her even more because I didn't want her to think she disgusted me.

"Momo . . . Momo . . ."

"Yes, Madame Rosa, it's me. Honest it is."

"Momo . . . I heard . . . They've called an ambulance . . . They're coming . . .''

"It's not for you, Madame Rosa, it's for Monsieur Bouaffa. He's dead already."

"I'm afraid . . ."

"I know, Madame Rosa. It proves you're alive."

"The ambulance . . ."

She had trouble talking, because words need muscles to get out and her muscles had all gone flabby.

"It's not for you. They don't even know you're here. I swear it by the Prophet. *Khaïrem.*"

"They're coming, Momo . . ."

"Not now, Madame Rosa. Nobody's denounced you. You're as alive as two kittens, look the way you've shat and pissed in your pants, you've got to be alive to do that."

That seemed to comfort her a little. I looked at her eyes to keep from seeing the rest of her. You won't believe me, but that old Jewish woman had eyes of perfect beauty. They were like Monsieur Hamil's carpets when he said: "I have carpets of perfect beauty." Monsieur Hamil thinks there's nothing more beautiful in the world than a beautiful carpet and Allah is sitting on it. If you ask me, Allah is sitting on an awful lot of things.

"You're right. It does stink."

"That proves you're working properly inside."

"*Insh'Allah,*" said Madame Rosa. "*Insh'-Allah* I'll die soon."

"*Insh'Allah*, Madame Rosa."

"I'll be glad to die, Momo."

"We're all glad for you, Madame Rosa. We're all your friends here. We all wish you well."

"But you mustn't let them take me to the hospital, Momo. Not for anything in the world."

"You needn't worry, Madame Rosa."

"In the hospital they'll keep me alive by force, Momo. They have laws. Regular Nuremberg laws. You don't know about those things, you're too young."

"I've never been too young for anything, Madame Rosa."

"Dr. Katz will denounce me to the hospital and they'll come and get me."

I didn't say anything. If the Jews were starting to denounce each other, I wasn't going to get mixed up in it. The Jews give me a pain, they're just people like anybody else.

"They won't abortion me at the hospital."

I still didn't say anything. I held her hand. That way at least I didn't tell any lies.

"That world champion in America, Momo. How long did they make him suffer?"

I played it dumb.

"What champion?"

"In America. I heard you. You were talking about him with Monsieur Waloumba."

Hell.

"Madame Rosa, they all have world's records in America, they're such big athletes. Here in France, like on the Saint-Etienne soccer team, it's all foreigners. They've even got Brazilians and God knows what. They won't take you. To the hospital, I mean."

"Swear it."

"As long as I'm here, Madame Rosa, the hospital is out."

She almost smiled. Between you and me, when she smiles, it doesn't improve her looks, on the contrary, because it draws attention to everything else. It's especially her hair that's missing. She still had thirty-two hairs on her head like the last time.

"Madame Rosa, why did you lie to me?"

She seemed sincerely flabbergasted.

"Me? Lie to you?"

"Why did you tell me I was ten when I'm fourteen?"

You won't believe me, but she blushed a little.

"I was afraid you'd leave me, Momo, so I depreciated you just a bit. You've always been my little man. I've never really loved anybody else. So I counted the years and I was afraid. I didn't want you to grow up too fast."

All I could do was kiss her. I kept her hand in mine and put my arm around her as if she were a woman. After a while Madame Lola came in with the oldest Zaoum brother and we lifted her up and undressed her and spread her out on the floor and washed her. Madame Lola poured perfume all over her, we put on her wig and her kimono, and laid her on her bed fresh and clean. She was a pleasure to behold.

BUT MADAME ROSA WAS DETERI-
orating fast and I can't tell you how unfair it is
that somebody should go on living just because
they're suffering. Her constitution had gone from
bad to worse and when it wasn't one thing it was
another. It's always the aged and defenseless that
get attacked; it's easier, and that's the kind of
crime wave that was happening to Madame Rosa.
All her organs were shot, the heart, the liver, the
kidneys, the lungs, not one was in Grade A condition. Only her and me were left in the apartment
and on the outside we didn't have anybody but
Madame Lola. Every morning I walked Madame
Rosa around to take the stiffness out of her bones.
We'd go from the door to the window and back
again, because if we hadn't she'd have rusted up
completely. During our walks I'd put on a Jewish
record she liked and that wasn't as sad as most.
The Jews always have sad records, I don't know
why. It's their folklore that does it. Madame Rosa
used to say that all her troubles came from the
Jews and nine tenths of them would never have
happened if she hadn't been Jewish.

Monsieur Charmette sent up a funeral wreath,
because he didn't know it was Monsieur Bouaffa
who had died. He thought it was Madame Rosa as

everybody wished for her own good, and Madame Rosa was pleased because it gave her hope and nobody had ever sent her flowers before. Monsieur Waloumba's tribal brothers brought bananas, chickens, mangoes and rice, which is their custom when a happy event is expected in the family. We all persuaded Madame Rosa that it would soon be over, and that way she wasn't so scared. Father André came to see her too, he was the Catholic priest who looked after the African lodging houses around the rue Bisson, but he didn't come as a priest, he just came. He was always very correct and never made any advances to Madame Rosa. We didn't argue with him either, because you know how it is with God. He does what He damn well pleases because He's got the big stick.

Father André has died in the meantime of a broken heart, but I don't think it was personal, I think it must have been the state of the world. I didn't tell you about him before because Madame Rosa and me weren't really in his department. They'd sent him to Belleville to look after the African workers who were Catholics, and we weren't either one or the other. He was very gentle and always looked kind of guilty, as if he knew something wasn't quite right in his business. I'm mentioning him now because he was a good man and his death left me with a pleasant memory.

It looked like Father André was going to stay a while, so I went down the street for the latest news because something horrible had happened in the neighborhood. The junkies called heroin "shit," so some little eight-year-old kid hears they get a kick from shooting themselves with shit. The next thing you know he shits in a newspaper and gives himself a shot of real shit, thinking it's the right kind, and naturally it kills him. They'd even arrested Le Mahoute and two other guys for giving him the wrong information, but if you ask me it wasn't exactly their duty to teach an eight-year-old kid the right way to give himself a fix.

When I got back upstairs, Father André had company, the rabbi from the rue des Chaumes next door to Monsieur Rubin's kosher grocery store. He must have heard that a priest was prowling around Madame Rosa and been afraid she'd die in the arms of the Church. He'd never set foot in our place before, seeing he'd known Madame Rosa ever since her whoring days. Neither Father André nor the rabbi, who had another name but I don't remember what, wanted to make the first move to get up and go, so they just sat there on two chairs next to Madame Rosa's bed. They even talked about the war in Vietnam, because that was neutral ground.

Madame Rosa had a good night but I couldn't sleep. I lay in the dark with my eyes open and thought about something different, except I had no idea what it was.

In the morning Dr. Katz came up to give Madame Rosa a check-up. And as soon as it was over we went out on the landing and I knew that calamity was creeping up to our door.

"She'll have to go to the hospital. She can't stay here. I'm going to call an ambulance."

"What will they do to her at the hospital?"

"They'll give her the proper care. She may go

on living for quite some time if not longer. I've seen persons in her condition prolonged for years."

Hell and damnation, I thought, but I didn't say anything in front of the doctor. I hesitated a moment. Then I asked:

"Look, Doctor, just between Jews, couldn't you abortion her?"

He seemed sincerely flabbergasted.

"What! Abortion her? What are you talking about?"

"That's right. Abortion her. To stop her suffering."

Dr. Katz was so overcome he had to sit down. He held his head in his hands and sighed several times in succession, raising his eyes to heaven as customary.

"No, my little Momo. We can't do that. Euthanasia is absolutely forbidden by law. We're living in a civilized country. You don't know what you're talking about."

"Oh yes, I do. I'm an Algerian. I know perfectly well what I'm talking about. In Algeria they've got the sacred right of peoples to self-determination."

Dr. Katz looked at me as if I'd scared him. His mouth was wide open and he didn't say a word. Sometimes I get good and sick of the way people refuse to understand.

"Do you believe in the sacred right of peoples, or don't you?"

"Of course I believe in it," said Dr. Katz. He even got up from the step he was sitting on to show his respect.

"Of course I believe in it, it's a good and fine thing. But I don't see the connection."

"The connection is that if you believe in it you'll have to admit that Madame Rosa has the sacred right of peoples to self-determine herself just like everybody else. If she wants to be abortioned, she has a perfect right. And *you* should do it for her because it's got to be a Jewish doctor to steer clear of anti-Semitism. Jews have no business making each other suffer. It's disgusting."

I spoke so well that Dr. Katz was breathing harder and harder and even had drops of sweat on his forehead. It was the first time I'd really been four years older.

"You don't know what you're saying, my child. You don't know what you're saying."

"I'm not your child, and I'm not a child in the first place. I'm the son of a whore and my father killed my mother. When a kid knows that, he knows everything there is to know and he's not a child any more."

Dr. Katz looked at me with stupefaction. He was trembling from top to toe.

"Who told you that, Momo? Who told you those things?"

"It doesn't matter who told me, Dr. Katz, because sometimes it's best to have as little father as possible, trust my long experience as I've had the honor, to talk like Monsieur Hamil, Monsieur Victor Hugo's old pal, who I'm sure is not without being unknown to you. And don't look at me like that, Dr. Katz, because I'm not going to have a fit of violence, I'm not psychiatric, I'm not hereditary, and I'm not going to kill my fucking mother because it's been done already, God keep her ass, which did lots of good on earth, and I shit on the whole lot of you except Madame Rosa, who's the only thing I've ever loved here below. I won't let you turn her into a world's champion vegetable for the pleasure of medical science, and when I write my *Misérables* I'll say everything I want to say without killing anybody because it's the same thing, and if you weren't a heartless old kike but a real Jew with a real heart instead of an organ you'd do a good deed and abortion Madame Rosa right this minute to save her from the life that was pumped into her ass by a father who's not even known and hasn't even got a face because he hides it, and you can't even get a picture of him because he's got a whole Mafia to keep him from getting caught, and the result is a crime wave against Madame Rosa, and all you crummy doctors should be sent to jail for refusing to help a person in . . .''

Dr. Katz was ashly pale, which went well with his nice white beard and his cardiac eyes, and I stopped because if he died he wouldn't have heard half of what I was going to tell them some day. But his knees were buckling and I helped him to sit down on the step, but I didn't forgive him for half a second. He pressed his hand to his heart and looked at me like a bank teller begging me not to kill him. But I only folded my arms over my chest and felt like a nation with the sacred right to self-determine itself.

''My little Momo, my little Momo . . .''

''I'm not your little Momo. Just tell me if it's yes or no?''

"I haven't the right . . ."

"You refuse to abortion her?"

"I can't. Euthanasia is severely punished."

He made me laugh. Can you think of anything that isn't severely punished, especially when there's nothing to punish?

"We've got to put her in the hospital. For humanitarian reasons . . ."

"Will they let me stay there with her?"

That almost reassured him. He even smiled.

"You're a good boy, Momo. No, but you can visit her. Only pretty soon she won't recognize you . . ."

He tried to change the subject.

"And by the way, what will become of you, Momo? You can't live alone."

"Don't worry about me. I know a pile of whores in Pigalle. I've had several offers."

Dr. Katz opened his mouth and looked at me and gulped and sighed like they all do. Meanwhile I was thinking. I needed to gain time. That's always the most important thing.

"Look, Dr. Katz. Don't call the hospital. Give me a few days. Maybe she'll die all by herself. Besides, I've got to make my arrangements. Otherwise they'll hand me over to the Public Welfare."

He sighed some more. The guy couldn't breathe without sighing. I was good and sick of people that sighed.

He stared at me again but with a different expression.

"You've always been different from other children, Momo. And you'll be different from other men. I've always known it.''

"Thank you, Dr. Katz. It's nice of you to say so.''

"I mean it. I'm convinced of it. You'll be entirely different."

I thought a moment.

"Maybe it's because I had a psychiatric father.''

Dr. Katz looked so sick I thought maybe he wasn't feeling well.

"Not at all, Momo. That's not what I meant at all. You're still too young to understand, but . . .''

"Nobody's ever too young for anything, Doctor, trust my long experience.''

That seemed to floor him.

"Where did you learn that expression?''

"That's what my friend Monsieur Hamil always says.''

"Oh. You're a very intelligent, very sensitive boy. Too sensitive in fact. I've often told Madame Rosa that you wouldn't be like other people. Sometimes youngsters like you grow up to be great poets and writers, and sometimes . . .''

He sighed.

''. . . and sometimes revolutionaries. But don't be alarmed. That doesn't mean you won't be normal.''

"I sure hope I'll never be that, Dr. Katz. Only real bastards are normal. God forbid!''

He stood up again and I thought it was time to ask him something that was beginning to bug me seriously.

"Tell me, Doctor, are you sure I'm fourteen? Are you sure I'm not twenty or thirty or even more? First the story is ten, then fourteen. Couldn't I be a lot more? Couldn't I be a midget, damn it all? I don't want to be a midget, Doctor, even if they are normal and different.''

Dr. Katz smiled in his beard. He was glad to have good news for me finally.

"No, Momo, you're not a midget. I give you my medical word. You're fourteen, but Madame Rosa wanted to keep you as long as possible, she was afraid you'd leave her. That's why she said you were only ten. Maybe I should have told you a little sooner, but . . .''

He smiled and that made him look even sadder.

". . . but because it was such a beautiful love story I didn't say anything. For Madame Rosa's sake I'm willing to wait a few days, but I'm convinced that she'll have to be hospitalized. As I've explained, we have no right to cut her suffering short. In the meantime make her exercise a little. Get her to stand up, move her limbs, walk around the room, because if you don't she'll rot all over and abscesses will form. A little exercise, understand? Two or three days. No more . . .''

I called one of the Zaoum brothers, who carried him downstairs on his shoulder.

Dr. Katz is still alive, and I'll go to see him one of these days.

I STAYED THERE AWHILE, SITTING ON
the stairs. I needed to think. It was good news
that I wasn't a midget, the first in a long time. I
once saw a picture of a basket case, somebody
without arms or legs. I often think of him because
then I feel better off than him and I get the full
pleasure of having arms and legs. Then I thought
about the exercises I'd have to give Madame Rosa
for her circulation, and I went to get Monsieur
Waloumba to help me, but he was working in the
garbage. I stayed all day with Madame Rosa, who
laid out the cards and read her future. When Monsieur Waloumba got home from his work, he came
up with his friends and they put Madame Rosa
through a little exercise. Her legs could still be
used, so first they walked her around the room.
Then they laid her down on a blanket and swung
her a little to shake her insides up. After a while
they started laughing because Madame Rosa
looked like a big doll and they seemed to be
playing some game. It did her a lot of good and
she even had a kind word for each one of them.
After that we put her to bed and fed her and she
asked for her mirror. When she saw herself in the
glass she smiled and fixed her thirty-five
remaining hairs a little. We all congratulated her

for looking so well. She made herself up. She still had her feminine side, there's no reason why even the ugliest people shouldn't try to fix themselves up nice. It's too bad Madame Rosa wasn't beautiful, because she'd have been a very nice-looking woman. She smiled at herself in the mirror and we were all very happy to see she wasn't disgusted.

Then Monsieur Waloumba's brothers made her rice with pimentos; they said she needed seasoning to stir up her blood. At that point Madame Lola arrived, and that Senegalese was always like the sun shining in. The thing that makes me sad about Madame Lola is when she dreams of having everything cut off in front to make her a real woman. That sounds like extremities to me, and I'm afraid it won't be good for her.

Madame Lola gave Madame Rosa one of her dresses, because she knew how important morale is for a woman. She brought us champagne too, because there's nothing better. She poured perfume on Madame Rosa, who needed it more and more, because she had trouble controlling her openings.

Madame Lola has a cheerful nature. She was blessed in that direction by the sun of Africa, and it was a joy to see her sitting on the bed with her legs crossed, dressed in the height of fashion. Madame Lola is very beautiful for a man except her voice, which dates from the day when she was a heavyweight champion. She couldn't help it because the voice is connected with the balls, which were the great tragedy of her life. I had Arthur the umbrella with me, I couldn't give him up over-night in spite of the four years I'd suddenly put on. Other people take a lot longer to put on four years, and I wasn't going to let anyone hurry me.

All this gave Madame Rosa such a shot in the arm that she managed to get up and even walk by herself. It was a moment of respite and hope. When Madame Lola went off to work with her handbag, we had a little dinner, and Madame Rosa ate the chicken that Monsieur Djamaili, the well-known grocer, had sent her. Monsieur Djamaili himself had deceased, but they'd had good relations in his lifetime and his family had taken over the business. Then she had a little tea with jam and started looking thoughtful. I was afraid she was starting a fresh attack of imbecility, but we'd shaken her up so much that day that her blood reported for duty and went to her head as planned.

"Momo, tell me the whole truth."

"Madame Rosa, I don't know the whole truth. I don't even know who knows it."

"What did Dr. Katz tell you?"

"He said we'd have to put you in the hospital and they'll take care of you and prevent you from dying. You can live a long time yet."

It made my heart ache to talk like that. I even tried to smile as if it was good news I was telling her.

"What do they call this sickness I have?"

I swallowed my saliva.

"It's not cancer, Madame Rosa, I swear it isn't."

"But what is it, Momo? What do the doctors call it?"

"You can live like that for years."

"Like what?"

I didn't answer.

"Momo, don't lie to me. I'm an old Jewish

woman. Whatever can be done to a man has been done to me.''

She said *mensh*. In Yiddish a man and a woman are the same.

"I want to know. Some things they have no right to do to a *mensh*."

"It's nothing, Madame Rosa. A person can perfectly well live like that."

"Like what, Momo?"

That was as much as I could stand. The tears were choking me inside. I ran over to her, she took me in her arms, and I shouted:

"Like a vegetable, Madame Rosa, like a vegetable! They want to make you live like a vegetable!"

She didn't say anything. She only perspired a little.

"When are they coming to get me?"

"I don't know. In a day or two. Dr. Katz is very fond of you, Madame Rosa. He says he won't separate us unless he has to."

"I won't go," said Madame Rosa.

"I don't know what to do, Madame Rosa. They're all such bastards. They refuse to abortion you."

She seemed very calm. She only wanted to wash herself, because she'd pissed in her pants.

She was beautiful, now that I think of it. It depends on the way you think of a person.

"It's the Gestapo," she said.

She didn't say anything after that.

I was cold during the night. I got up and put another blanket over her.

I woke up happy the next day. When I first

wake up in the morning, I don't think of anything and that makes it nice for a while. Madame Rosa was alive. She even gave me a pretty smile to show everything was all right. She only had a pain in her liver, which was hepatic, and in her left kidney, which Dr. Katz wasn't too pleased with, and various other details that were out of order, but don't ask me what they were, because they're not in my department. The sun was shining outside, and I opened the curtains to let in the benefit, but she didn't like it because with all that light she saw too much of herself and it made her sad. She took the mirror and said:

"Oh, Momo, I've gotten to be such a fright."

That made me angry, because it's not right to say mean things about a woman who's old and sick. In my opinion you can't judge everything by the same standards, like turtles and hippopotamuses, for instance, because they're just not the same as other people.

She closed her eyes and some tears flowed out, but I don't know if she was crying or it was just her muscles letting go.

"I'm hideous. You can't fool me."

"Oh, Madame Rosa, it's just that you're not the same as other people."

She looked at me.

"When are they coming for me?"

"Dr. Katz . . ."

"Don't talk about Dr. Katz to me. He's a good man but he doesn't understand women. I was beautiful once, Momo. I had a first-class clientele on the rue de Provence. How much money have we got left?"

"Madame Lola slipped me a hundred francs yesterday. She'll give us more. Her business is thriving."

"I'd never have worked in the Bois de Boulogne. There's no place to wash. At Les Halles we had comfortable hotels with hygiene. Besides it's dangerous in the Bois de Boulogne because of the sex maniacs."

"Madame Lola doesn't have to worry about sex maniacs. She just socks them on the jaw. She was a boxing champion, remember?"

"She's a saint. I don't know where we'd have been without her."

Next she wanted to recite a Jewish prayer like her mother had taught her. I was scared, I thought she was dropping off into second childhood, but I didn't want to cross her. The trouble was she couldn't remember the words because of the softness in her brain. She'd taught Moïse that prayer and I'd learned it too, because it made me feel bad when they did things without me. So I recited:

"Shema Yisroel adenoi eloheinu adenoi ekhod borukh shein kveit malkhusseh loeilem bowet . . ."

She said it over with me and when we'd finished, I went to the can and spat three times *ptoo ptoo ptoo*, like the Jews, because it wasn't my religion. Then she said she wanted to get dressed, but I couldn't help her by myself, so I went to the black lodging house next door and brought back Monsieur Waloumba, Monsieur Sokoro, Monsieur Tané and some others, I can't tell you all their names, because they're all very nice over there.

THE MINUTE WE GOT BACK I SAW
Madame Rosa's screws had come loose again, her
eyes were glassy and she was salivating with her
mouth open as I've had the honor and would
rather not repeat. I remembered what Dr. Katz
had said about giving Madame Rosa exercises to
shake her up and make the blood rush to all the
places that need it. We laid her down on a blanket
and Monsieur Waloumba's brothers picked her up
with their proverbial strength and started shaking
her, but at that moment Dr. Katz arrived on the
back of the oldest Monsieur Zaoum, with his
medical instruments in a small valise. He flew into
a raving lather before even getting down off the
oldest Monsieur Zaoum's back, because that
wasn't what he meant at all. I'd never seen him in
such a temper. He even had to sit down and hold
his heart, because all the Jews here are sick, they
came to Belleville from Europe a long time ago,
they're old and tired, and that's why they stopped
here and couldn't go any further. He bawled me
out something awful and called us all a lot of
savages, which offended Monsieur Waloumba,
who said such remarks were ungracious. Dr. Katz
apologized and said he hadn't meant to be
pejorative, but he'd never told anybody to toss

Madame Rosa in the air like a pancake, only to walk her around the room with slow and infinite care. Monsieur Waloumba and his tribesmen put Madame Rosa into her armchair, because the sheets needed changing on account of her natural requirements.

"I'm going to call the hospital," said Dr. Katz definitively, "and tell them to send an ambulance at once. Her condition demands it. She needs constant care."

I started bawling but I knew it wouldn't do any good. And that's when I had a brilliant idea, because I was capable of anything.

"Dr. Katz," I said. "We can't send her to the hospital. Not today. Not with her family coming."

He seemed surprised.

"What? Family? But she's all alone in the world."

"She has family in Israel and . . ."

I swallowed my saliva.

"They're arriving today."

Dr. Katz observed a minute of silence in memory of Israel. He couldn't get over it.

"I didn't know that," he said, and now there was respect in his voice, because for the Jews Israel is something.

"She never told me . . ."

Things were looking up. I was sitting in a corner with my overcoat and Arthur the umbrella. I took Arthur's derby hat and put it on for the *baraka*, which means luck to us Arabs.

"They're coming to get her today. They're taking her to Israel. It's all arranged. The

Russians have given her a visa."

Dr. Katz was dumbfounded.

"The Russians? What are you talking about?"

Damn. I could see I'd gotten something twisted. But I distinctly remembered Madame Rosa saying you needed a Russian visa to go to Israel.

"Anyway, you know what I mean."

"You're mixing things up a bit, my little Momo, but I see . . . So they're coming to get her?"

"Yes, they heard she was losing her mind, so they're taking her to live in Israel. They're taking the plane tomorrow."

Dr. Katz was stroking his beard with amazement, it was the best idea I'd ever had. For the first time I was really four years older.

"They're very rich. They own a lot of big stores and they're motorized. They . . ."

Hey, I said to myself, don't lay it on too thick.

". . . they . . . well, they're loaded."

"Tss, tss," went Dr. Katz, wagging his beard. "That's good news. The poor woman has suffered so . . . But why didn't they show up sooner?"

"They wrote her to come, but Madame Rosa didn't want to leave me. Madame Rosa and I can't live without each other. We're all we've got in the world. She wouldn't want to walk out on me. Even now she doesn't want to. Only yesterday I had to get down on my knees. Madame Rosa, go to your family in Israel. You'll die peacefully, they'll take care of you. Here you're nothing. There you'll be much more."

Dr. Katz stared at me. His mouth was wide

open. Some emotion even spread to his eyes. They were slightly moist.

"It's the first time an Arab has ever sent a Jew to Israel," he said. It came as such a shock he could hardly get the words out.

"She didn't want to go without me."

Dr. Katz looked thoughtful.

"Couldn't both of you go?"

That hit me hard. I'd have given anything to go somewhere.

"Madame Rosa said she'd ask when she got there."

I was so short of anything to say next that I hardly had any voice left.

"She finally accepted. They're coming to get her today and tomorrow they'll all take the plane."

"And what about you, my little Mohammed? What will become of you?"

"I've found somebody here until I send for myself."

"Until . . . what?!"

I didn't say another word. I'd gotten myself into a beautiful mess and I didn't know how to get out of it.

Monsieur Waloumba and his tribe were really happy, because it was plain that I'd fixed everything up. I was sitting on the floor with Arthur my umbrella. I'd lost all track of where I was at and I didn't even want to know.

Dr. Katz stood up.

"Well, that *is* good news. Madame Rosa may live for quite some time, though she probably won't know it very often. She's sinking fast. But in her moments of consciousness she'll be glad to look around and see she's with her own people. Tell her family to stop in and see me. I never go out any more, you know."

He put his hand on my head. The number of people that put their hands on my head is unbelievable. It does them good.

"If Madame Rosa recovers consciousness before she leaves, give her my congratulations."

"I sure will. I'll tell her *mazel tov* for you."

Dr. Katz looked at me with pride.

"You must be the only Arab in the whole world that speaks Yiddish, my little Momo."

"I guess so. *Mehdornisht zorgen.*"

Which in case you don't know Yiddish means: we can't complain.

"Don't forget to tell Madame Rosa how glad I am for her," Dr. Katz repeated, and this is the last time I'll mention him to you because life is like that.

The oldest Monsieur Zaoum was waiting politely at the door to carry him down. Monsieur Waloumba and his tribal brothers put Madame Rosa into her nice clean bed. Then they left too. And I sat there with Arthur my umbrella and my overcoat, looking at Madame Rosa, who was lying on her back like a big turtle that wasn't made for it.

"Momo . . ."

I didn't even look up.

"Yes, Madame Rosa."

"I heard everything."

"I know. I noticed your eyes."

"So I'm going to Israel?"

I didn't say anything. I kept my head down because every time we looked at each other we made each other feel bad.

"You did right, my little Momo. You'll help me, won't you?"

"Of course I'll help you, Madame Rosa, but not now, not right away."

I cried a little.

SHE HAD A GOOD DAY AND SHE SLEPT
well that night but the morning after our trouble
was even worse because the rent hadn't been paid
for months and the house agent came around. He
said it was disgraceful to keep a sick old woman in
an apartment with nobody to take care of her and
we should put her in an asylum for humanitarian
reasons. He was fat and bald with eyes like
roaches and when he left he said he was going to
call the La Pitié Hospital for Madame Rosa and
the Public Welfare for me. He also had a big
wiggly moustache. I galloped down the stairs and
caught him in Monsieur Driss's café, where he was
just going to telephone. I told him that Madame
Rosa's family was coming next day to take her to
Israel, and I said I was going with her so the apartment would be his for the taking. Then I had a
brainstorm. I told him Madame Rosa's family
would pay him the three months' rent we owed
and the hospital wouldn't pay him anything.
Which goes to show that the four years I'd gotten
back made a big difference and I was making giant
strides in the art of thinking. I even pointed out
that if he sent Madame Rosa to the hospital and
me to the Public Welfare he'd have every Jew and
Arab in Belleville on his ass for obstructing our

return to the land of our ancestors. And while I
was at it I promised him that he'd wake up one
morning with his *khlawi* in his mouth because
that's what the Jewish terrorists always do, and
they're the worst devils going except for my Arab
brothers who are fighting to self-determine themselves and go back home, and between me and
Madame Rosa he'd have the sum total of Jewish
and Arab terrorists on his ass and he'd better start
counting his balls. Everybody was watching us
and I was congratulating myself on my Olympic
form. I wanted to kill the guy, I was desperate,
and nobody had ever seen me like that at the café.
Monsieur Driss was listening, and he advised this
house agent not to get mixed up in embroilments
between Jews and Arabs, because he'd wish he
hadn't. Monsieur Driss is a Tunisian, but they've
got Arabs there too. The house agent was as white
as a sheet. He said he hadn't known we were going
home and nobody would be gladder than he was.
He even asked me to join him in a drink. It was the
first time anybody had ever offered me a drink
like a man. I ordered a Coke. Then I said so long
and went back up the six flights. There wasn't a
moment to lose.

I FOUND MADAME ROSA IN HER STATE
of stupor, but it was easy to see she was afraid and
that's always a sign of intelligence. She even
pronounced my name like she was calling for help.

"Here I am, Madame Rosa, here I am . . ."

She was trying to say something. Her lips
moved, and her head trembled, she was trying
hard to be a human being. But nothing much came
of it, only her eyes got bigger and bigger and she
sat there with her mouth wide open and her hands
on the arms of her chair, looking straight ahead as
if she could already hear the doorbell . . .

"Momo . . ."

"Don't worry, Madame Rosa. I won't let them
take you to the hospital and turn you into the
world's champion vegetable . . ."

I don't know if I've told you that Madame Rosa
still had her portrait of Monsieur Hitler under her
bed. When she felt really bad, she'd take it out
and look at it, that always picked her up. I pulled
out the portrait and put it under Madame Rosa's
nose.

"Madame Rosa, Madame Rosa, look who's
here . . ."

I had to shake her. She sighed a little. Then she
saw Monsieur Hitler's face and it didn't take her

long to recognize him. She let out a yell, which revived her and she tried to get up.

"Quick, Madame Rosa, we've got to be going."

"Are they here?"

"Not yet, but we have to leave. We're going to Israel, remember?"

She started functioning, because in old people memories are always the strongest.

"Help me, Momo . . ."

"Easy does it, Madame Rosa. Plenty of time. They haven't phoned yet, but we can't stay here . . ."

I had a hard time dressing her, and to make things worse she insisted on fixing herself up, and I had to hold the mirror while she was painting her face. It was beyond me why she had to be her Sunday best just then, but you can't argue with a woman's female nature. She had a pile of finery in her closet that didn't look like anything ever seen, she'd bought the stuff at the Flea Market when she was in the chips, not to put on but to dream over. The only thing the whole of her would fit into was her Japanese-type kimono all covered with birds, flowers and the rising sun. It was red and orange. She also put her wig on. Then she wanted to look at herself in the mirror, but I didn't let her, I thought I'd better not.

It was eleven o'clock that night before we started down the stairs. I'd never have thought she could make it. How could anybody suspect how much strength Madame Rosa had left when it came to dying in her Jewish hideaway? I'd never believed in this Jewish hideaway. I'd never realized what she'd fixed it up for and why she went down there from time to time and sat down and looked around her and breathed. Now I understood. I hadn't lived enough yet to have enough experience, and even now talking to you I know that even after years of taking it on the chin there's always something left to learn.

There was something wrong with the minute-light and it kept going out. On the fifth floor we made some noise and Monsieur Zidi, who came from Oujda, looked out to see what was going on. When he saw Madame Rosa, his mouth froze open as if he'd never seen a Japanese-type kimono and he closed the door quick. On the fourth floor we passed Monsieur Mimoun, who sells peanuts and chestnuts in Montmartre and is going back home to Morocco soon, having made his fortune. He stopped and looked up.

"Good God, what's that?"

"It's Madame Rosa. She's going to Israel."

He thought it over. Then he thought it over some more, and his voice was still scared stiff when he asked:

"Why have they dressed her like this?"

"I don't know, Monsieur Mimoun. I'm not Jewish."

Monsieur Mimoun gulped.

"I know the Jews. They don't dress like that. Nobody dresses like that. There's no such thing."

He took out his handkerchief and wiped his forehead. Then he helped Madame Rosa down, because he saw it was too much for one man by himself. Down at the bottom he asked me where her luggage was and wouldn't she catch cold waiting for the taxi. He even got sore and started yelling that it wasn't right sending a woman to the Jews in such a state. I told him to climb the six flights and talk to Madame Rosa's family, who were taking care of the luggage, and he left me, saying the last thing in the world he wanted to get mixed up with was sending Jews to Israel. So then we were alone on the ground floor, and we had to hurry because it was still half a flight down to the cellar.

When we got there Madame Rosa collapsed in the armchair and I thought she was going to die. She'd closed her eyes and her breathing wasn't strong enough to lift her chest. I lit the candles and sat down on the floor beside her and held her hand. That improved her a little, she opened her eyes and looked around.

"Momo," she said. "I knew I'd need it some day. Now I can die in peace."

She even smiled.

"I won't win the world's vegetable record."

"*Insh'Allah.*"

"Yes, Momo, *insh'Allah.* You're a good boy, Momo. We've always been happy together."

"Oh yes, Madame Rosa. You've got to admit it's better than nobody at all."

"And now help me say my prayer, Momo. Maybe I'll never be able to say it again."

"*Shema Yisroel adenoi . . .*"

She repeated the whole thing with me up to *loeilem bowet* and seemed happy. After that she had a good hour but then she deteriorated again. During the night she mumbled in Polish because of her childhood there. She kept saying the name of some guy by the name of Blumentag that maybe she'd known as a procurer when she was a woman. Then she didn't say anything at all, just sat there looking empty at the wall and shitting and pissing in her chair.

There's something I've got to tell you. Such things shouldn't be. That's my honest opinion. I'll never understand why abortion is only allowed for the young and not for the old. In my opinion the guy in America who beat the world's vegetable record was worse than Jesus, because he stayed on the cross for seventeen years and then some. In my opinion there's nothing crummier than ramming life down the throats of defenseless people who've had enough.

There were lots of candles and I lit a whole pile of them to keep it from being too dark. Blumentag, Blumentag, she muttered twice more. He was beginning to get on my nerves. I'd have liked to see her Blumentag knocking himself out for me the way I was for her. But then I remembered that *blumentag* means day of flowers in Yiddish, so it must have been some female dream she was having. There's nothing stronger than a woman's female nature. She must have gone to the country once when she was young, maybe with some guy, and it stayed with her.

"Blumentag, Madame Rosa."

I left her a while and went back upstairs for Arthur my umbrella, because I was used to him. And later on, I went up another time for the portrait of Monsieur Hitler, which was the only thing that still had any effect on her.

I didn't expect Madame Rosa to stay in her Jewish hideaway for long, I thought God would take pity on her, because when you're at the end of your rope you get all sorts of crazy ideas. I looked at her beautiful face now and then and I finally remembered that I'd forgotten her makeup and all the stuff she used to make herself look like a woman, and I went back up a third time. To tell you the truth, I was getting sick of it, really, she wanted too much.

I put the mattress next to her for company but I couldn't shut an eye because of the rats, which have a bad reputation in cellars, but there weren't any. I don't know when I fell asleep, but when I woke up hardly any of the candles were burning. Madame Rosa's eyes were open, but when I put the portrait of Monsieur Hitler in front of them she wasn't interested. It was a miracle that we made it down there in her condition.

IT WAS NOON WHEN I WENT OUT. I hung around on the sidewalk and when anybody asked me how Madame Rosa was getting along I said she'd gone to her Jewish home in Israel, her family had come for her and in Israel she'd have conveniences and would die much faster than here in Belleville, which was no life for her. Or maybe she'd live a while and then she'd send for me, there was no law against it, Arabs could go there too. Everybody was glad she had found peace. I went to Monsieur Driss's café. He fed me for nothing and I sat down across from Monsieur Hamil, who was sitting by the window in his beautiful gray and white djellaba. He couldn't see at all any more as I've had the honor, but when I told him my name three times he remembered right away.

"Ah yes, little Mohammed, yes yes, I remember . . . I know him well . . . What has become of him?"

"It's me, Monsieur Hamil."

"Oh, it's you. Forgive me. I've lost my eyesight."

"How are you, Monsieur Hamil?"

"I had a good dish of couscous yesterday, and for lunch today I'm having chicken soup. I haven't been told what there will be this evening, I'm curious to know.''

He still had his hand on Monsieur Victor Hugo's Book and he looked far into the distance as though trying to discover what he would have for dinner that night.

"Monsieur Hamil, is it possible to live without someone to love?''

"I love couscous, my little Victor, but not every day.''

"You misunderstand me, Monsieur Hamil. When I was little you told me a person couldn't live without love.''

His face lit up from the inside.

"Yes, yes, it's true. I loved someone too when I was young. Yes, you're right, my little . . .''

"Mohammed. Not Victor.''

"Yes, my little Mohammed. When I was young, I loved someone. I loved a woman. Her name was . . .''

He stopped. He seemed surprised.

"I don't remember.''

I got up and went back to the cellar. Madame Rosa was in her state of stupor. I was feeling rotten, I ached all over. I put the portrait of Monsieur Hitler in front of her eyes again, but it left her cold. I thought maybe she'd live like this for years and I didn't want to afflict it on her, but I was afraid to abortion her myself. Even in the darkness she didn't look good, so I lit all the candles I could for company. I spread some makeup on her lips and cheeks and painted her eyebrows the way she liked. I made her eyelids blue and white and pasted little stars on them like she did. I

tried to put on false eyelashes but they wouldn't
stick. I could see she'd stopped breathing, but it
was all the same to me, I loved her even without
breathing. I lay down beside her on the mattress
with Arthur my umbrella and tried to feel even
worse because then I'd have been completely
dead. When the lights went out around me I lit
more and more candles. They burned out several
times. Then the blue clown came to see me in spite
of my four extra years and put his arm around me.
I ached all over and the yellow clown came too. I
dropped the four years I'd gained, I didn't care
about them any more. Once in a while I'd get up
and hold the portrait of Monsieur Hitler in front
of Madame Rosa's eyes, but it didn't mean a thing
to her, she wasn't with us any more. I kissed her
once or twice, but that didn't help either. Her face
was cold. She was beautiful with her artistic
kimono, her red wig, and all the makeup I'd
spread on her face. I put on a little more here and
there because she looked kind of gray and blue
every time I woke up. I slept on the mattress
beside her and I was afraid to go out because
nobody was there. All the same I went up to
Madame Lola's, because she was different. But
she wasn't home. It wasn't the right time. I was
afraid to leave Madame Rosa alone, because
maybe she'd wake up and think she was dead if
everything was black all around her. I went back
down and lit a candle but only one, because she
wouldn't have liked to be seen in the state she was
in. I had to paint her again with lots of red and
other nice colors to keep her from seeing what she

looked like underneath. I slept some more beside
her, then I went up again to see Madame Lola. She
really wasn't like anybody else. She was shaving
and she'd put on some music and fried eggs that
smelled good. She was half naked and rubbing
herself hard to take away the traces of her work.
Seeing her naked like that with her razor and her
shaving foam, she didn't look like anything under
the sun that made me feel better. When she
opened the door for me, I'd changed so much in
four years that it took her breath away.

"Oh my God, Momo! What's the matter? Are
you sick?"

"I've come to say good-by for Madame Rosa."

"Have they taken her to the hospital?"

I sat down because I hadn't the strength to
stand. I hadn't eaten since God knows when, I was
on a hunger strike. I don't give a shit for the laws
of nature. I don't even want to know what they
are.

"No, not to the hospital. Madame Rosa is in
her Jewish hideaway."

I shouldn't have said that. But I saw right away
that Madame Lola didn't know where it was.

"What?"

"She's gone away to Israel."

That got such a surprise out of her that she
stood with her mouth open in the middle of the
lather.

"She never said anything to me about going
away."

"They've come for her by plane."

"Who's come?"

"The family. She's got a lot of relatives there. They've come to get her by plaine with a car at her disposal. A Jaguar."

"And she's left you all alone?"

"I'm going too. She's sending for me."

Madame Lola looked at me some more and touched my forehead.

"Why, Momo. You've got a fever."

"Don't worry. I'm all right."

"Come and eat with me. It'll do you good."

"No, thanks. I've stopped eating."

"What, stopped eating? What are you talking about?"

"I don't give a shit for the laws of nature, Madame Lola. I'm through with them.

That made her laugh.

"So am I."

"I say fuck the laws of nature, they're no good, they stink on ice and they shouldn't be allowed."

I stood up. She had one breast higher than the other because she wasn't natural. I liked her fine.

She gave me a sweet smile.

"How about coming to live with me in the meantime?"

"No thanks, Madame Lola."

She squatted down beside me and took my chin in her hands. Her arms were tattooed.

"You can stay here. I'll take care of you."

"No, thanks, Madame Lola. I've already got somebody."

She sighed, and then she stood up and went and rummaged in her handbag.

"Here, take this."

She slipped me three hundred francs.

I went and turned on the water faucet, I was as thirsty as a lord.

I went back down and shut myself up with Madame Rosa in her Jewish hideaway. But I couldn't take it. I took all the perfume that was left and poured it on her, but it was still impossible. I went out to the rue Coulé and bought some paint, a lot of different colors, and then I ran to Monsieur Jacques, the well-known perfumer, who's a heterosexual and is always making advances at me, and bought several bottles of perfume. I'd decided to punish everybody by not eating anything, but by that time I was so mad I woudn't even speak to them anymore so I ate a couple of hot dogs at a bar. When I got back, Madame Rosa smelled even stronger and I poured on a bottle of Samba perfume, which was her favorite. Then I painted her face all different colors to hide it as much as possible. Her eyes were still open, but with the red, green, yellow and blue around them they didn't look so horrible because there wasn't anything natural about them any more. Then I lit seven candles the way the Jews always do and lay down beside her on the mattress.

It's not true that I spent three weeks with the corpse of my adoptive mother, because Madame Rosa wasn't my adoptive mother. It's not true, and I couldn't have stood it because I hadn't any perfume left. I went out four times to buy perfume with the money Madame Lola had given me and I stole as much again. I poured it all over her and I painted and repainted her face all the colors I had to hide the laws of nature, but she was decaying something terrible all over because there's no pity. When they broke down the door to see where it came from and saw me lying beside her, they started yelling help how awful, but they hadn't thought of yelling sooner because life has no smell. They took me away in an ambulance and found the piece of paper with your name and address. They thought there was some connection between us, so they called you up because you've got a telephone. So then you all came and took me to stay with you in the country with no obligation on my part. I think Monsieur Hamil was right when he had his brains that it's not possible to live without someone to love, but I don't promise you anything, we'll have to wait and see. I loved Madame Rosa and I'll keep going to see her. But I don't mind staying with you a while, seeing your kids have asked me and it was Madame Nadine who showed me how to make the world go backwards. I really go for that and I sure wish it would. Dr. Ramon even went and got Arthur my umbrella. I was worried about him because nobody'd want him for his sentimental value, it takes loving.